William Thomas Pyke

Australian Heroes and Adventurers

William Thomas Pyke

Australian Heroes and Adventurers

ISBN/EAN: 9783337179465

Printed in Europe, USA, Canada, Australia, Japan

Cover: Foto ©Andreas Hilbeck / pixelio.de

More available books at **www.hansebooks.com**

ROBERT O'HARA BURKE.

PYKE'S AUSTRALIAN SERIES.

AUSTRALIAN HEROES

AND

ADVENTURERS.

LONDON:

WALTER SCOTT, 24 WARWICK LANE.

MELBOURNE: E. W. COLE, BOOK ARCADE.

1889.

PREFACE.

THIS book is the first of a series which I intend to publish, illustrative of life and adventure in the Australian Colonies and the Islands of the Pacific. It has been carefully compiled from reliable sources of information—viz., *Wills's Diary*, *King's Narrative*, *Howitt's Diary*, Wood's *Explorations in Australia*, Withers's *History of Ballarat*, Sutherland's *Tales of the Gold-fields*, Raffello's *Account of the Ballarat Riots*, McCombie's *History of Victoria*, etc., etc. I may mention that most of these books are very expensive or out of print, and therefore not easily procurable at the booksellers.

In the succeeding volumes of the series I propose to give—"Buckley, the Runaway Convict, and his Black Friends," "John Batman, the Founder of Melbourne," "Fawkner, the Pioneer," "Early Days of Tasmania," "Botany Bay Tales," "Remarkable Convicts," "Notorious Bushrangers," "Brave Deeds," "Squatting Tales," "Remarkable Personal Adventures," "Curious Anecdotes," etc., etc.

WILLIAM THOMAS PYKE.

MELBOURNE.

CONTENTS.

—————•◦•—————

Burke and Wills—Two Heroes of Exploration.

Old Times on the Gold-Fields.

Contents.

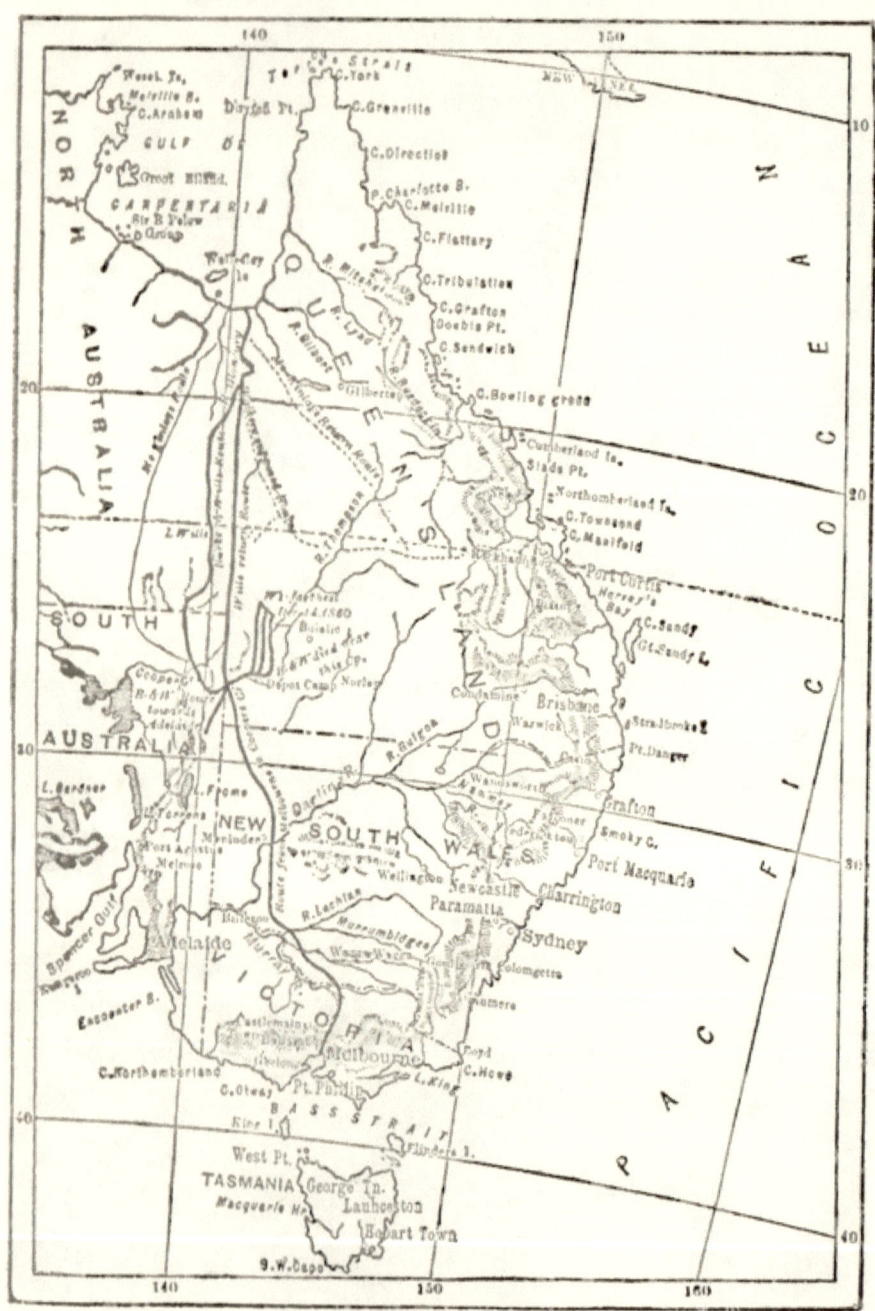

MAP ROUTE.

BURKE AND WILLS.

TWO HEROES OF EXPLORATION.

CHAPTER I.

ACROSS AUSTRALIA.

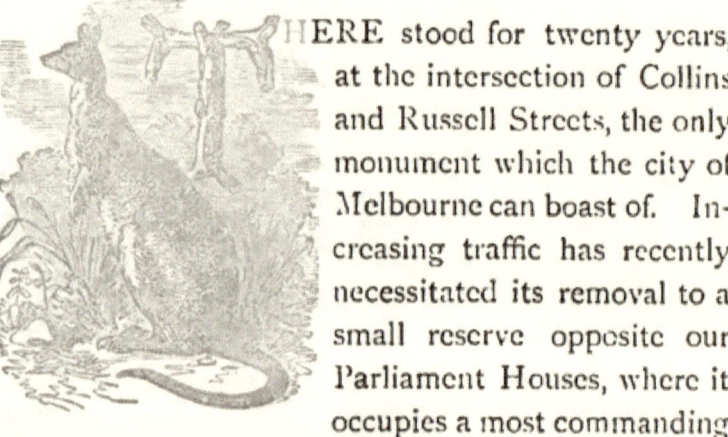

HERE stood for twenty years, at the intersection of Collins and Russell Streets, the only monument which the city of Melbourne can boast of. Increasing traffic has recently necessitated its removal to a small reserve opposite our Parliament Houses, where it occupies a most commanding position at one of the chief entrances of the city. It is the lasting memorial of two men and the expedition they led across the continent of Australia. It stands in silent and solemn grandeur amidst the noisy turmoil of a busy thoroughfare—two massive figures gazing earnestly and longingly, seemingly in a solitude as complete as the deepest seclusion of the lonely plains of the interior, where the heroes whose memory they perpetuate met their fate. No inscription tells the curious visitor or wayfarer who they are, or records the deeds that have gained them such a high place in the estimation of the citizens of Victoria. The story is an old one in these days of rapidly passing events, but we think it will bear repetition, and, therefore, in the following pages we will do our best to relate the events that led to the erection of so magnificent a memorial.

From the days of the first settlement of New South Wales at Port Jackson in 1788, down to the present time, the laudable desire of bettering their condition, enhanced by the adventurous spirit moving in their breasts, has prompted the colonists of Australia to organise parties for the exploration of the unknown interior of their vast continent. In not a few instances the explorer has been the precursor of the squatter and the selecter of settlements and civilisation. The journey of Oxley, in 1818, led to the discovery that the Macquarie and other rivers ended in large reedy marshes. This discovery gave rise to the belief in an immense inland sea, into which all the rivers of the interior emptied themselves. But subsequent travellers in search of this supposed inland sea dissipated the belief in its existence. In 1828 Sturt reached the "great salt river," called the Darling, which has since filled such an important part in facilitating the carriage of our staple product to the ocean. In his next journey Sturt went down the Murrumbidgee and the Murray as far as Lake Alexandrina. His description of the country surrounding the lake—plenty of green pastures and abundance of agricultural land of the most fertile kind—induced the squatters to send down their emaciated flocks from the parched plains of Riverina, and also led to the emigration of numbers of farmers and vine-growers from overcrowded Europe, who founded the Colony of South Australia. Mitchell, in 1836, descended the Darling, crossed over the Murray, and entered into what is now the Colony of Victoria. He named it "Australia Felix," because the country which met his view delighted him with its beautiful scenery, and its congenial climate presented such a pleasant contrast to that of the land he had just travelled over. Pioneers from Port Jackson and Van Diemen's Land migrated to this newly-revealed district. The productiveness of its soil, and the subsequent discovery of gold, soon attracted a great number of adventurers and immigrants to the happy clime. In an incredibly short period the district grew into a rich and prosperous colony, and Melbourne, its mighty capital, took rank amongst the chief cities of the world.

The success attending the early exploring expeditions equipped by the mother colony seems to have incited the colonists of Victoria to emulate the doings of their neighbours. In 1859 a patriotic offer was

made by an enterprising citizen of Melbourne—
Mr. Ambrose Kyte—to contribute £1000 towards
defraying the cost of fitting out an expedition to
explore the vast interior of Australia. This generous
offer was accepted. The project was taken up by
the Royal Society of Victoria, and the sum of £3400
was raised by public subscription. The Government
voted £6000, and granted an additional £3000 for
the purchase of camels in India. Thus originated,
under the most favourable auspices, the Victorian
Exploring Expedition, which is now more commonly
known, owing, no doubt, to its calamitous termination, as the " Burke and Wills' Expedition."

The Exploration Committee had some trouble in
obtaining a suitable leader. Several well-known
explorers were written to, but each of them declined.
At last the appointment was given to Mr. Robert
O'Hara Burke, a man of approved ability, and in
himself actuated by an enthusiastic desire to perform
the hitherto unaccomplished feat of crossing our vast
continent from sea to sea.

Mr. Burke was an Irishman, born in 1821, and was,
therefore, only forty years old at the time of his
melancholy end. He had served in the Austrian
Cavalry, and also in the Irish Mounted Constabulary,
previous to his arrival in Van Diemen's Land, in
1853. After performing services as Acting Inspector
at Hobart Town and as Police Magistrate at Beechworth (Victoria), he was granted leave of absence in

order to go to England, where he hoped to obtain a commission in one of the regiments embarking for the seat of the war then waging between England and Russia. Being unsuccessful, owing to the termination of the war, he returned to Victoria, and shortly received an appointment as one of the superintendents of the Victorian Police Force, which position he held until the setting out of the exploring expedition. Mr. Burke diligently prepared himself for the journey across the continent. He examined the records of previous expeditions for the personal experiences of former explorers, as well as for knowledge of the interior already at hand. He also made severe walking tours, in order to qualify himself physically for the unusual hardships accompanying such a journey. The following characteristic letter, written whilst *en route*, will show his determination to succeed in his undertaking :—

" ON THE DARLING, *4th October* 1860.

" MY DEAR S——,

"I received your letter, and was glad to hear of the safe arrival of your friend B——. We have been resting here a few days, awaiting the arrival of the baggage, which has just come up. To-morrow we proceed on, and I shall not delay anywhere until I reach Cooper's Creek—being an Irishman I must add, unless I can't help it.

"I leave the hired waggons and my own behind. The accursed impediments, the ruin of so many expeditions, I am determined shall not ruin me.

"We all march on foot three **or four** hundred miles at all events, and **the camels and horses will have to** carry our weight in provisions.

"We **have** already done **so for the last forty** miles. **You** should have seen old B——'s **face, upon my** announcing that all the officers would have **to act as** working men, and that we should only carry 30. **lbs weight of** baggage for each man.

"Loading camels **and then marching twenty miles is no joke.** The first two days **of it nearly choked poor** B——, **and I think he will not be able to** stand **it much longer.**

"I am still confident of **success, and willing to accept the** alternative of success or disgrace, **although failure is possible.** This **self-imposed task** (as you **justly call it)** is no sinecure, and I think **will take the** sting **out of me if I see** it out. Good-bye, my **dear S——.**

"From yours, ever sincerely,

"R. O'HARA BURKE."

In William **John Wills we see the** real hero of the expedition. **He was** an Englishman, born in Devonshire, and at **his untimely end** was **but** twenty-seven **years of** age. He was **endowed** with an unquenchable thirst for knowledge. **It** manifested **itself on** the voyage out, where, **in addition to** his other studies, he acquired **a** knowledge **of the** science of navigation. After **his** arrival **in** Victoria, **in 1853, his** taste **for** science, which **was** also accompanied by a naturally courageous and enterprising spirit, displayed itself. At first he obtained an appointment in the Survey Department. He gained **a** knowledge of astronomical and other sciences **to** which the Observatory **is**

WILLIAM JOHN WILLS.

From Photo—HILL, Melbourne.]

2

dedicated, and was then admitted, through the influence of the Surveyor-General, into that establishment as an assistant. As early as 1855 the friends of young Wills had frequently heard him speak of his intention to explore the unknown interior of Australia, and to be one of the first to reach the shores of the Gulf of Carpentaria. In 1856 a proposal was mooted to send out an expedition, and, on hearing of this, Mr. Wills walked from the river Wannon to Ballarat, a distance of ninety miles, to offer his services ; but the project was abandoned. His scientific attainments had qualified him for an important post in the expedition of 1860, and he joined it in the capacity of astronomical and meteorological observer. Of his fitness for exploring, the Rev. Julian Woods writes—" Having studied every journal connected with Australian exploration, and become, as it were personally acquainted with all our discoverers, I conscientiously say I have not met with so courageous, so noble, so fine an explorer as William John Wills."

The other officers of the expedition were :—Mr. Landells, who had brought the camels to the colony, and was appointed second in command ; Dr. Herman Beckler, botanist and medical adviser of the expedition ; and Dr. Ludwig Becker, artist, naturalist, and geological surveyor. There were eleven subordinates, including three Hindoo camel-drivers.

On the 20th August 1860 the expedition left Melbourne. During the morning of its departure crowds

of holiday folks were to be seen wending their various
ways to the Royal Park, on the northern outskirts of
the city.   It was late in the afternoon before the
picturesque groups of camels and horses, with their
keepers and the baggage, were arranged in marching
order.   Then Mr. Burke, on a little grey horse, took
up his position at the head of the procession.   When
it was about to start, the Mayor of Melbourne
mounted one of the drays and delivered a short
speech, wishing them God-speed.   Mr. Burke un-
covered, and replied, in a clear voice that was heard
all over the crowd :—" Mr. Mayor, on behalf of myself
and the expedition, I beg to return you my most
sincere thanks.   No expedition has ever started
under such favourable circumstances as this.   The
people, the Government, the Committee—all have
done heartily what they could do.   It is now our
turn ! and we shall never do well till we justify what
you have done in showing you what we can do."
Then, amidst the loud cheering and acclamations of
the spectators, who numbered fully ten thousand, the
brilliant cavalcade was put in motion.   It was truly a
fine, imposing spectacle, and the applauding cheers
of the enthusiastic citizens were prolonged till the
procession had faded away in the dim distance.

The progress of the explorers through the settled
districts to the river Darling was very slow, and even
before they reached Menindie serious dissensions had
broken out in their camp.   On arriving at that town-

COOPER'S CREEK.

ship Burke dismissed the foreman, and Mr. Landells resigned his position and left the party. Mr. Wills was then appointed second in command, and instead of Mr. Landells, Burke placed in charge of the camels a man named Wright, whom he had picked up at a sheep station.

The Exploration Committee had instructed Burke to establish a depôt on Cooper's Creek, and make a line of communication between it and the Darling. When the explorers reached that river the spring season was far advanced, and soon the fervid rays of the sun would wither the green grass and dry up the water-courses ; therefore Burke decided to push forward to the creek without delay. But some of the camels were unfit to proceed immediately, so Burke divided his party, and with seven of his companions and Wright, who offered to show him a direct and well-watered track, set out from Menindie on the 19th of October.

They accomplished more than half of the journey, and having been fortunate in finding good feed and water on the way, Burke sent Wright back to the encampment on the Darling with instructions to bring the rear party with the heavy supplies on by easy stages to Cooper's Creek. On the 11th of November, thirteen days after despatching Wright, Burke and his party arrived safely at the creek. They then travelled slowly along the banks of the stream, recruiting the animals and looking around for a camping-ground. On the twenty-first they pitched on a suitable locality, and there established the main depôt.

Whilst awaiting the arrival of Wright with the remainder of the company, frequent excursions were made in order to find a route to the north. On one of these excursions, Mr. Wills travelled ninety miles without finding water; their camels escaped from them, and he and his companions were forced to return on foot. Fortunately for them they found a pool on their way back to the depôt, but the camels were never recovered. On another occasion Wills and King got into a stony desert. The knowledge obtained by means of these and other short excursions was not of an encouraging nature to the explorers.

After waiting at Cooper's Creek for more than a month, the advance party grew tired of their life of inaction, and made preparations for the journey to the Gulf of Carpentaria. As Wright did not come forward as expected, Burke got impatient, and decided to subdivide the few men he had with him as follows :—Four men were to remain at the depôt, one of them named William Brahé in command ; and were to construct a stockade while waiting for Wright, and when he had arrived they were to seek a more available and direct route to the Darling. The rest of the little party—Burke, Wills, King, and Gray—were to push forward to the Gulf, and were to take with them six of the camels, one horse, and three months' provisions.

On 16th December the little band of explorers bade their companions good-bye, and started northwards. As they proceeded, Burke and Wills walked ahead, while Gray and King followed behind, leading the horse and the six camels. Burke himself seldom wrote, but Wills, every evening after taking astronomical observations, wrote his diary, and then read it to Burke, who made such alterations in it as he thought necessary. Their allowance of provisions were a pound of flour and a pound of meat daily, with a little rice occasionally, and the party camped out every evening without tents. In his admirable history of the *Exploration of Australia,* a work published in 1865, and containing, in addition to the adventures of the explorers, a very lucid description of the physical features of the continent, so far as they had been made known by the journeys and discoveries previous to the year 1863, the Rev. Mr. Woods writes in reference to this journey :—" No doubt this self-denying mode of proceeding was very heroic and courageous, but was it necessary? It certainly does seem a pity that after the great care taken to equip the party adequately, that its main work should have been done by a feeble party, badly provisioned, and subject to the disadvantage of crossing the country on foot. The work was done, it is true, but done in an imperfect way. No one could

expect four poorly-fed men to manage six camels, to
force their way through untrodden scrubs, and yet
keep a journal and make observations. No one
could expect it, and it was not done. The journal
left is most incomplete, and to this day several
portions of the route are still matters of dispute."

For some distance the exploring quartette travelled
over well-watered country. Numerous parties of
natives were met with, but they were friendly to the
whites. Mr. Wills writes of a tribe of these :—
"They pestered us to go to their camp and have a
dance, which we declined. They were very troublesome, and nothing but a threat to shoot them will
keep them away. They are, however, easily frightened ; and although fine-looking men, decidedly not
of a warlike disposition. They show the greatest
inclination to take whatever they can, but will run no
unnecessary risk in so doing. They seldom carry
any weapon except a shield and a large kind of
boomerang, which I believe they use for killing rats,
etc. Sometimes, but very seldom, they have a large
spear ; reed spears seem to be quite unknown to
them. They are undoubtedly a finer-looking race of
men than the blacks on the Murray and Darling, and
more peaceful ; but in other respects I believe they
will not compare favourably with them. They
appear to be mean-spirited and contemptible in
every respect." After the explorers had passed
through this fertile country, they had to cross about

J. A. KING.

twenty miles of stony desert. On the other side of it they came upon an earthy plain of about nine miles. Then another nine miles of travelling through swampy plains brought them to the banks of a magnificent stream. The four men followed up this creek from point to point of the bends, and on the 7th of January camped well within the tropics. Afterwards they entered upon immense fertile plains, with innumerable creeks coursing through them, on the banks of which gum and box-trees and splendid grass grew luxuriantly. Pigeons and wild ducks were also found in abundance. For five days the travellers marched over these flourishing plains. Then they crossed over a series of low sandstone hills, and after passing over a stony plain came upon a range of mountains, which they called the Standish Ranges. On 27th of January the explorers reached Cloncurry Creek, one of the derivative streams of the river Flinders. They had afterwards to travel over swampy ground; the camels could not be got along, so all of them were abandoned. On the 9th of February, King and Gray were left behind with the bulk of the provisions, while Burke and Wills, taking the horse with them to carry supplies sufficient for three days, pushed forward towards the sea. They had to cross over patches of swampy ground; a great deal of it was so soft and rotten that the horse got bogged, and it was only by digging him out that he could be extricated. After great difficulty and delay they managed to do

this. Then they came across some tableland, and
beyond that a plain covered with water, which in
some places reached up to their knees. After wading
through several miles of this swamp, they came again
to dry land. Further on they met a few natives, who,
on seeing the explorers, decamped immediately,
leaving behind in their hurried departure some yams,
which were at once appropriated to appease the sharp
hunger of Burke and Wills. A small distance beyond
they reached a narrow inlet on the shore of the Gulf
of Carpentaria. A forest of Mangroves intercepted
their view of the open sea beyond, so the two heroic
men attempted to advance through it. The horse
had by this time become too weak to advance further,
therefore they hobbled him, and hastened forward
without him. But the two gallant fellows were soon
obliged to relinquish their attempt to pierce the thick
undergrowth. They could not obtain a view of the
open ocean, although they made every effort to do so.
'Tis true their mission was accomplished ; they had
crossed the continent to within a mile or two of its
northern shore—the victory was gained ! But now
the necessities of the case compelled the triumphant
explorers to immediately hurry back to Cooper's
Creek.

CHAPTER II.

THE RETURN JOURNEY.

THE two leaders returned to King and Gray on the 12th February 1861. The explorers soon afterwards recaptured all the camels, which had been greatly improved in condition by their rest. The remainder of the return journey was singularly disastrous. At first the progress was very much retarded by the incessant rain that deluged the whole country. Sickness commenced with Gray, and then Burke suffered a severe attack of dysentry, owing to his having eaten of the flesh of a large snake that he had killed. Their provisions became sadly reduced, and one camel, then another, had to be killed, in order to eke out their scanty supplies. On 6th of March one of the camels became bogged, and they were compelled to leave it. On the 20th, 60 lbs. of baggage were abandoned. They killed another camel on the 30th, and on the 6th of April they killed the horse, which had by this time become so weak that it could scarcely stand upright. By the 13th of April they had got back again to the Stony Desert. All were now nearly exhausted by their continued privations, but they slowly marched on in the hope of meeting assistance before they reached the depôt. On the 16th they, with poor Gray strapped to the back of a camel almost as emaciated as himself, managed to travel seven miles ; but during the night the unfortunate fellow succumbed under his extreme sufferings. His surviving companions, too, were all so weak in body that they could scarcely scratch a grave in the desert deep enough to cover his body. These three gaunt, emaciated, and sorrow-stricken beings rested but for a day, and then started afresh on their lonesome and weary journey, abandoning everything except the two camels, the fire-arms, and a little meat. On the 20th they made a tremendous effort by travelling all night, Burke riding one camel, and Wills and King the other. All next day they struggled manfully on, expecting soon to rest their aching limbs and worn-out bodies in the camp at Cooper's Creek. But on reaching the place where they had left the depôt party, instead of seeing the white tents of the camp gleaming in the rays of the declining sun, they saw nothing but the stockade now deserted by its former occupants. *There was no one there!* On looking eagerly around their eyes fell on the word DIG, cut in the bark of a tree. They anxiously turned up the soil, and unearthed a small parcel of provisions and a bottle containing a letter from Brahé, in which the disappointed men read with sinking hearts that he and his party had left the depôt *only that very morning.* The document ran thus :—

> "Depôt, Cooper's Creek, *April* 21*st*, 1861.
>
> "The depôt party of the V.E.E. leaves this camp to-day to return to the Darling. I intend to go S.E. from camp 60 deg., to get into our old track near Bulloo. Two of my companions and myself are quite well ; the third, Patten, has been unable to walk for the last eighteen days, as his leg has been severely hurt when thrown by one of the horses. No one has been up here from the Darling. We have six camels and twelve horses in good working condition.
>
> "WILLIAM BRAHE."

This was appalling news to the brave explorers, who, with their more than four months' severe travelling and unparalleled privations, were almost paralysed, and so exhausted that the slightest exertion produced in their pain-racked bodies such sensations of torture and utter helplessness as to render them more fit for a hospital than any further efforts on their part whatever. We will now leave the three abandoned men to recover from the first shock of their bitter disappointment, while we relate the circumstances that prevented the depôt party remaining at their post.

Previous to departing from Cooper's Creek, Burke sent a despatch to the Exploration Committee. In it he writes :—"I have every confidence in Brahé. The feed is good. There is no danger to be apprehended from the natives. There is nothing, therefore, to prevent the party remaining here until our return, or until their provisions run short." Burke's verbal instructions to Brahé were very indefinite. He led him to understand that the depôt party should remain at Cooper's Creek for three months, and that if the advance party did not return within that time the camp could be broken up, and Brahé and his party would be at liberty to quit the creek.

Brahé waited for four months and five days. The natives were troublesome for the most of the time, and confined the party to the camp. The men began to sicken and complain of scurvy, and as Wright with the rest of the company and provisions did not make an appearance, Brahé deemed it prudent to retrace the route from the Darling. His party went very slowly the first day, and camped a few miles down the creek. Had the ill-fated explorers of Burke's party known this and followed on their track, in all probability the fatal consequences of this desertion would have been avoided. It is deplorable to think that the three haggard men did not know that the other party were so near, and that after partaking of a hearty supper they slept all that night within a few miles of their returning companions.

Burke, Wills, and King rested for a couple of days at the abandoned depôt. The change of diet worked wonders in improving their strength and cheering their depressed spirits, and on the 23rd of April they felt equal to the task of resuming their journey.

Burke's plan was that they should make for Adelaide, by way of Mount Hopeless (an ill-omened name), where there was a large sheep station, and which he thought could not be further than one hundred and fifty miles off. Wills urged that they should return the way they came ; the distance to the Darling certainly was greater, being three hundred and fifty miles, but they were sure of feed and water all the way. Unfortunately for them all, as events afterwards proved, Wills yielded to Burke's decision, and the little party started for the mount. As they were about to leave the depôt, Burke deposited in the câche a letter from which we extract the following :— "We have discovered a practical route to Carpentaria, the chief portion of which lies on the 140th meridian of east longitude. There is some good country between this and Stony Desert. From there to the tropics the country is dry and stony. Between the tropics and the gulf a considerable portion is rangey, but is well watered and richly grassed. We reached the shores of the Gulf of Carpentaria on the 11th of February." Their starting day was fine, and the agreeable warmth of the weather lent fresh hopes to the three men as they marched slowly along the green banks of the creek. They were still further elated by meeting with a few well-behaved blacks, who gave them good supplies of fish in exchange for some straps and matches. On the sixth day they had a mishap—one of the camels became bogged

beside a water-hole. They attempted to place boughs
and timber beneath him, but he sank too rapidly;
and being of a sluggish, stupid nature, could not make
sufficiently strenuous efforts towards extricating himself. They then let in water from the creek so as
to buoy him up and soften the mud around his legs,
but it was of no avail; the brute lay there as if enjoy-
ing himself. The next day they shot the beast dead,
cut off as much of his flesh as they could, and then
dried it in the sun. The following day the natives
very liberally presented them with a quantity of fish
and cake; the explorers returned the compliment
by giving them fish-hooks and some sugar. After
leaving the blacks, the three men struck a southerly
branch of Cooper's Creek, which they traced down
till its channel broke up into small water-courses, and
was at last lost in the sand. Then for two days they
travelled, looking around for some other stream,
but finding none, Burke and Wills left King with
the camel, and pushing ahead, found that the soil
became loose and cracked up; and as it appeared to
be more parched further south, they returned to
King.

The prospects of the little party now looked
gloomy. Their provisions were rapidly diminishing;
their clothing, and especially their boots, all going
to pieces; and their only remaining camel, which
had been ailing for some time, now showed signs
of being done up. But the two leaders determined

On the March.

to examine the creek more closely, and after a short rest they set out again.

They came across some natives who were fishing. The blacks, probably moved by the forlorn appearance of Burke and Wills, gave them half of the fish just caught, and promised further supplies if they would come with them to their camp. On reaching it the almost destitute explorers were treated most generously—lumps of nardoo cake and handfuls of fish were forced on them till they could positively eat no more. The hospitable blacks also offered them some stuff composed of dried stems and leaves of shrubs, which, when chewed even in small quantities, was highly intoxicating. The poor travellers could only show their gratitude to the benevolent blacks by tearing off and giving them two pieces of cloth from their tattered macintoshes. Burke now returned to King, while Wills continued for seven miles along the creek until it tended northwards; then he returned, passing through the blacks' camp on his way to rejoin his companions. The natives invited him to stay, and he was again hospitably entertained. After supplying him with fish and nardoo cake, they brought him a couple of rats baked in their skins. Poor Wills must have been hungry, for he says " the rats looked nice and were most delicious." Supper over, one of the natives offered to share his gunyah with the weary traveller, and all of them were very attentive in bringing wood and keeping up the fire during the night. Early next morning Wills parted from his black friends.

When he rejoined Burke and King he found them jerking the flesh of the camel, for the poor beast had become so weak and helpless that they had been obliged to shoot it. The three men now despaired of reaching the settled districts. The only prospect before them was to wander about the creek, living like the blacks until the arrival of a relief party. So Burke and King went in search of the natives' camp for the purpose of ascertaining where the seed grew from which the natives made their bread, and also to find their mode of preparing it. Wills remained behind jerking the camel's flesh. In his diary he cheerfully writes that he must devise some means of trapping the birds and rats, but expresses deep regret at being obliged to hang about the creek after having made such a dashing trip to the Gulf of Carpentaria.

On reaching the spot where the blacks had camped, Burke and King found the place deserted, so they came back to Wills. The three dejected men moved irresolutely in the direction of where the blacks had been. Then Burke thought it better for one of them to go back and stop with the things for a few days, so that he might get the benefit of the remains of the camel's flesh, whilst the other two should go forward in search of the blacks and the nardoo. Accordingly, Burke and King took four days' provisions and left Wills at the junction, preparing for a final effort on their return. The two unfortunate men could not find the blacks, so it was settled that the party should abandon their cumbrous baggage and make another effort to reach Mount Hopeless.

The next day, 17th of May, King found the nardoo plant. This discovery revolutionised the feelings of the weary explorers. Poor Wills, cheerful even in this extremity, records the fact with the observation that they were now in a position to support themselves without the aid of the blacks. Collecting the seeds was a slow and troublesome work, and the three men were fully occupied in it for seven days.

This plant, the seeds of which answer the purposes of flour among the natives, grows in little tufts close to the ground. It resembles clover, but is quadrifoliate instead of trifoliate, and its leaves are covered with a silver down, which is also found on the seeds when fresh. These grow upon separate short stalks springing from the roots, and are flat and oval. The gathering of them is generally done by the native women, who, after cleaning the sand from them and pounding them between two stones, bake the flour into cakes.

The little party travelled for three days, tracing a water-course until it lost itself in the flat country. Travelling then became very fatiguing ; over dreary plains they struggled along almost exhausted. At last, from sheer exhaustion, they were obliged to relinquish the attempt to reach the mountain. They took an hour's rest, and then wearily retraced their steps.

In two days they reached the nearest water of the creek, and lay down their worn-out bodies under the cool shade of the box-trees growing on its fertile banks. For a meal, they boiled some of the nardoo seeds, and then made for the main creek. They came across some native huts, in one of which they found a pounding-stone left by the blacks. The poor explorers found the work of pounding the seeds so very slow and troublesome that they were compelled to mix half flour with the badly-ground seeds. The three men afterwards went back to their last camp and brought up all the dried meat they had planted there, and then remained at the deserted gunyahs, gathering and pounding nardoo seeds, and living as best they could. Whilst the poor fellows are thus living on the lower part of Cooper's Creek we will leave them, and turn back in order to find out the causes of Wright's delays.

When Wright returned to Menindie he heard that McDonall Stuart, the South Australian explorer, had almost crossed the continent. Wright thought his leader ought to know of this, so that if his own route should fail he could turn westward, strike Stuart's track, and continue the exploration northward. Two of the men and a native were sent out in the vain hope of overtaking Burke and informing him of this new discovery, but they lost their way, and sent the native back to Menindie with a slip of paper imploring assistance. A relief party was sent out by Wright. The two men were found living with the blacks about one hundred and ninety miles away, and were brought back to Menindie on 19th of December. Wright now proved his utter unfitness for his responsible position by remaining on the Darling for more than a month after the return of this party. On 26th of January he set out for Cooper's Creek, but proceeded so leisurely that it was the 12th of February before he reached Torowotto, the place where Burke and he had separated three and a half months before. It was now the hottest time of the year, and the summer sun had dried up all the surrounding country excepting the permanent creeks. Dr. Beckler and three of the men became seriously ill with the scurvy, and Wright erected a tent for them at Koorliatto Creek, about twenty miles from Bulloo. He then made for Bulloo, and from thence attempted to reach Cooper's Creek, a distance of between seventy and eighty miles ; but in consequence of the hostility of the natives he was unable to finish his journey, and was forced to return. Dr. Beckler and the three men were removed to Bulloo, and reached it on the 21st of April, the day on which Burke and his two companions arrived at the deserted depôt. A few days afterwards two of the sick men died. The natives had by this time become very troublesome, and the party were compelled to build a stockade. At last

they had to open fire upon them in order to disperse
them. Rats also abounded at the place, and did
considerable damage, even attacking the men.

On the 29th of April Wright was astonished to see
Brahé and the returning depôt party, and to hear
from them that they had neither seen nor heard
anything of the advance party for more than four
months. On the evening of the same day Dr. Beckler
died, and next day was buried. Wright was un-
decided how to act—first he thought of returning to
Menindie, and turned back to Koorliatto Creek ; but
when there he thought it possible that the advance
party might have returned to the depôt, so he and
Brahé left his party in the encampment and made
for Cooper's Creek.

On the 8th of May, while Burke and his two
companions were down at the lower part of the creek
making for Mount Hopeless, Wright and Brahé
arrived at the depôt, and seeing the place undisturbed
they concluded that the advance party had perished
in the journey northwards. Wright and Brahé made
a terrible blunder in not digging to see if the
provisions deposited by Brahé had been removed.
After a careless look around they returned to the
encampment at Koorliatto, and then the whole party
set out for the River Darling. Their progress was
slow, and another fatality occurred near Torowotto.
On the 6th of January, Patten, who had been
gradually sinking since he left the depôt with Brahé,

succumbed under his privations. Wright's party reached the Darling on the 18th of June, and immediately sent despatches to the Exploration Committee, begging that search might be made for the advance party.

CHAPTER III.

WE will now take up the thread of the narrative from where we left the enfeebled explorers (Burke, Wills, and King) at the deserted gunyahs. They adopted the life of the blacks, and managed to subsist on the nardoo, although it was very innutritious. More than a month had elapsed since they had left the depòt, and Burke thought that a relief party might have reached that place in the interval. Wills now volunteered to return and deposit, in place of Burke's former note, a letter stating that the party were living on the lower part of the creek, and also to bury there the field-books of the journey to the Gulf. He expected to be away for eight days, and took with him three pounds of flour, four pounds of pounded nardoo, and one pound of dried meat.

During his absence Burke and King had the following adventure with the blacks (we have copied the account of it from King's narrative):—"A few days after Mr. Wills left, some natives came down the creek to fish at some water-holes near our camp.

They were very civil to us at first, and offered us some fish ; the second day they came again to fish, and Mr. Burke took down two bags, which they filled for him ; the third day they gave us one bag of fish, and afterwards all came to our camp. We used to keep our ammunition and other articles in one hut, and all three of us lived together in another. One of the natives took an oil-cloth out of this hut, and Mr. Burke seeing him run away with it, followed him with his revolver and fired over his head, and upon this the native dropped the oil-cloth. While he was away, the other blacks invited me away to the water-hole to eat fish ; but I declined to do so, as Mr. Burke was away, and a number of natives were about who would have taken all our things. When I refused, one took his boomerang and laid it over my shoulder, and then told me, by signs, that if I called out for Mr. Burke as I was doing he would strike me. Upon this I got them all in front of the hut and fired a revolver over their heads, but they did not seem at all afraid until I got out the gun, when they all ran away. Mr. Burke, hearing the report, came back, and we saw no more of them until late that night, when they came with some cooked fish and called out, 'White fellow!' Mr. Burke then went out with his revolver, and found a whole tribe coming down, all painted, and with fish in small nets carried by two men. Mr. Burke went to meet them, and they wished to surround him, but he knocked as many of the nets of fish out of their hands as he could, and shouted out to me to fire. I did so, and they ran off. We collected five small nets of cooked fish. The reason he would not accept the fish from them was that he was afraid of being too friendly, lest they should be always at our camp." While Burke was cooking some of the fish during a strong wind, the flames caught the gunyah, and spread so rapidly that the two men were unable either to extinguish them or to save any of their things, except one revolver and a gun.

How the heroic Wills fared on his lonely journey is described in the following extracts taken from his diary :—

On the 27th of May he came upon three black gins and some children collecting nardoo, which was so abundant in some places that the ground was quite covered with it. The native women directed him to their camp, and he was soon afterwards overtaken by about twenty blacks, who were bent upon taking him to it, promising him nardoo and fish. One carried his shovel, another insisted in such a friendly manner on taking his swag that Wills could not refuse. They were greatly amused with various little things he had. In the evening he partook of a supper of fish and nardoo, and one of the old men shared his gunyah with poor Wills. The night was very cold. Next morning he felt the friendly blacks. During the day he felt very unwell. On the 29th the tottering man saw some crows quarrelling about something near the water. He found it to be a large fish. The crows had eaten a large portion of it, but he, finding it fresh and good, decided the quarrel by eating the remainder of it. The fish proved a valuable addition to his otherwise scanty meal of nardoo porridge. That night he slept in a very comfortable mia-mia, about eleven miles from the depôt. On the 30th of May he reached his destination, but found no trace of anybody except the blacks having been there, although Wright and Brahé had visited the place only twenty-two days before, at the time when Burke and himself were being treated so generously by the blacks on the lower part of the creek. He deposited the journals and a notice stating the wretched condition of himself and companions. Next day he started on his return journey, although his exertions had made him very tired and weak. In the evening he camped under some bushes in a sheltered gully, thinking he would reach the blacks' camp next day. But next day he felt altogether too weak and exhausted, and had extreme difficulty in getting across numerous small gullies, and soon was obliged to stop and rest himself. The following morning at 6.30 he again started, thinking to break-fast with the blacks, but found himself so very much fatigued that he did not arrive at their camp till ten o'clock ; but his expectations of receiving a

good breakfast were disappointed, for the camp was
by this **time deserted.** He rested **here awhile, and**
breakfasted **off a few fish-bones which** the **blacks**
had left. The disappointed man then started down
the creek, hoping by a late march to reach his companions, **but soon found this** was **out of the question.**
By good luck he came across a large fish, about a
pound and a half in weight, being choked by another
which it had tried to swallow, but which had stuck
in its throat. The hungry man soon made a fire,
and had both fish cooked and eaten. He was
awakened **next morning by the encouraging** sounds
of cooeys, then fancied he saw smoke in the distance ;
and was afterwards set at ease by hearing a cooey
from **one of his former black friends, who** also continually repeated **assurances of bread** and fish. With
some difficulty the weary **man** managed **to** ascend
a sandy path leading **to** the natives' **camp.** He was
conducted by the chief **to** the fire, where there was
a large **pile of** fish cooked in the **m**ost approved
style. He imagined it was for general consumption
by the half-dozen natives who had gathered round;
but it turned out they had all eaten, and expected
Wills to dispose **of it** all. He set to work at the
task, and to his **own** astonishment accomplished it
by keeping two **or** three blacks steadily **at** work
extricating the bones for him. Fish finished, then
came **a** supply of nardoo cake **and** water, till he
was so full that he was unable to eat any more. The

native who called Wills to the camp allowed him a short time to recover himself, and then filled a large bowl with raw nardoo flour, and mixed it into a thin paste. This mixture is a most insinuating article to the blacks, and esteemed by them as a great delicacy. They then invited Wills to stop, but he declined ; although, he says, he would have liked to have stopped and lived with them in order to learn something of their ways and manners. He continued his return journey, and on the 6th of June reached Burke and King.

The three men had been so well treated by the blacks that they now decided on shifting their camp nearer to them, and set out with such things as they could carry, but found themselves very weak, in spite of the abundant supplies of food they had lately had. Poor Wills could scarcely get along, although carrying the lightest swag (about 30 lbs.). They found that the blacks had decamped from the place where Wills had last seen them, so they moved on to the camp near the nardoo field. The almost exhausted men managed to reach the nardoo field, but, greatly to their disappointment, no blacks were there. The explorers took possession of the best mia-mia and rested.

Until the 24th of June these unfortunate men lived on the field, going out daily to gather the nardoo, and then returning to the hut in order to clean and pound the seeds. After eating the last

piece of dried camel's flesh, they found that although
the nardoo was in abundance, it was so innutritive that
by itself it could not support them. Wills it would
not sustain at all, and the poor young man wrote
in his diary: "I am determined to chew tobacco
and eat less of the nardoo." Burke, after a few
days, showed signs of caving in. King managed
to live on the nardoo; it seemed to agree with him
better than with his companions. However, Wills
became so weak as to be unable even to crawl about,
and on the 24th wrote: "Little chance of anything
but starvation unless we get hold of some blacks."

The little clothing they had could not keep out
the cold, and during the nights they suffered terribly
from it. Wills' wardrobe consisted of a wide-awake
hat, merino shirt, regatta shirt without sleeves,
remains of a pair of flannel trousers, and a waist-
coat, of which he had managed to keep the pockets
together. His companions were better off. The
three men had with them for bedding—two small
camel pads, some horsehair, two or three little bits
of rag, and pieces of oil-cloth saved from the fire.

It is impossible to imagine the state of mind these
three unfortunate men were then in. The expedition
that ended so disastrously for them had started ten
months before with the most brilliant prospects, and
now three of its members were on the point of starvation and dying of fatigue. Unless they received
assistance very soon, the three men must undoubtedly

perish. After consulting together it was agreed that Wills should be left alone in the gunyah, while his two companions went in search of the blacks. With great reluctance the two men packed up food enough to last them a couple of days, but hesitated at leaving their dying companion. They repeatedly desired his candid opinion, and he again and again urged them to go, saying, "It is our only chance." After placing the nardoo and firewood near his bed, Burke and King sorrowfully took leave of him ; and then, tottering along like two worn-out beggar-men, they set out in search of succour.

Wills maintained the uniformity of his cheerful disposition, and the last entry in his diary, written without a complaint a few days before he expired, moves us to admiration of his fine, manly qualities. Here it is :—" I am weaker than ever, although I have a good appetite and relish the nardoo much, but it seems to give us no nutriment, and the birds here are so sly as not to be got at. Even if we could get fish, I doubt whether we could do much on that and nardoo alone. Nothing now but the greatest good luck can save any of us. As for me, I may live four or five days if the weather continues warm. My pulse is at forty-eight and very weak, and my legs and arms are nearly skin and bone. I can only look out, like Mr. Micawber, for something to turn up. Starvation on nardoo is by no means unpleasant, but for the weakness one feels and the utter inability to move one's self. As for my appetite, it gives me the greatest satisfaction. Certainly, fat and sugar would be more to one's taste ; in fact, these seem to be the great stand-by in this extraordinary continent. Not that I mean to deprecate farinaceous food, but the want of sugar and fat in all substances obtained here makes them become almost useless to us as articles of food without the addition of something else." Soon after (perhaps a few hours) the departure of his companions, the hand of death put an end to the sufferings of poor Wills. It was a terribly hard fate for one so young and full of promise to meet there in the lonely wilderness, without the sympathetic and encouraging presence of a friendly voice to break the mournful silence, with no gentle hand to administer the last kind soothing offices of humanity.

Let us now follow the two remaining sufferers. In travelling the first day Burke seemed very weak, and complained of great pain in his back and legs. Next day he seemed better, and said he thought he was getting stronger ; but on starting did not get more than two miles, when he found he could go no further. King persisted in his trying to go on, and managed to get him along several times, until Burke was almost knocked up. He said he could not carry his swag, and threw all he had away. King did likewise, and took nothing but a gun, some powder and shot, a small pouch, and some matches. They did not go far before Burke said they should halt for the night.   King prevailed on him to go a little further on to a less exposed spot, where they camped. King searched about and found a few small patches of nardoo.   He collected and pounded some of the seeds, and with a crow which he had shot, the two worn-out men made a good evening's meal.   From the time they halted Burke grew worse, and, although he ate his supper, said he felt convinced he could not last many hours.   He gave King his watch and pocket-book, and also wrote some notes.   He then said, " I hope you will remain with me here till I am quite dead.   It is a comfort to know that some one is by ; but when I am dying it is my wish that you should leave my pistol in my right hand, and that you leave me unburied as I lie."   That night he spoke very little.   On the following morning he was speech-less, or nearly so, and about eight o'clock he expired. Thus the gallant Burke ended his brave and noble career.   King saw there was no use remaining there any longer, and wandered about in the most forlorn condition.   " I felt very lonely," he says.   We can well imagine that, and everything around must have sadly reminded him of his late companions in mis-fortune.   He wandered up the creek in search of the natives, and at night usually slept in deserted wurleys belonging to them.   Two days after leaving the spot where Burke died he came across some gunyahs, in one of which the natives had left a bag of nardoo sufficient to last the hungry man a fortnight.   After

remaining there two days he returned to Wills, taking
back with him two crows which he had shot.

On his arrival King found that his fellow-sufferer,
whom he had grown to love so dearly, was lying dead
in the hut, and that the natives had been there and
taken away some of the clothes.   He buried the
corpse, and remained a few days.   Then, as his stock
of nardoo was getting low, and he was unable to
gather any more, he tracked the natives that had
been in the camp by their footprints in the sand some
distance down the creek, shooting crows and hawks
on the road.   Soon he came up to the blacks, and
afterwards kept with them until rescued by the relief-
party.   How he lived we learn from his own
narrative :—

"The natives, hearing the report of the gun, came
to meet me, and took me with them to their camp,
giving me nardoo and fish.   They took the birds I
had shot, and cooked them for me, and afterwards
showed me a gunyah, where I was to sleep with
three of the single men.   The following morning they
commenced talking to me, and putting one finger on
the ground and covering it with sand, at the same
time pointing up the creek, saying, 'White fellow,'
which I understood to mean that one white man was
dead.   From this, I knew that they were the tribe
who had taken Mr. Wills's clothes.   They then asked
me where the third white man was, and I also made
the sign of putting the fingers on the ground, and

AUSTRALIAN ABORIGINES.

covering them with sand, at the same time pointing up the creek. They appeared to feel great compassion for me when they understood that I was alone on the creek, and gave me plenty to eat. After being four days with them, I saw that they were becoming tired of me, and they made signs that they were going up the creek, and that I had better go downwards; but I pretended not to understand them. The same day they shifted camp, and I followed them ; and on reaching their camp, I shot some crows, which pleased them so much that they made me a shelter in the centre of their camp, and came and sat round until such time as the crows were cooked, when they assisted me to eat them. The same day one of the women, to whom I had given part of a crow, came and gave me a ball of nardoo, saying that she would give me more, only she had such a sore arm that she was unable to pound. She showed me a sore on her arm, and the thought struck me that I would boil some water in the billy, and wash her arm with a sponge. During the operation the whole tribe sat around, and were muttering one to another. The husband sat down by her side, and she was crying all the time. After I had washed it, I touched it with some caustic, when she began to yell and ran off, crying, ' Mokow ! mokow !' (Fire ! fire !). From this time she and her husband used to give me a small quantity of nardoo both night and morning, and whenever the tribe were about going on a fishing

excursion, he used to give me notice to go with them.
They also used to assist me in making a shelter
whenever they shifted camp. I generally shot a
crow, or a hawk, and gave it to them in return for
these little services. Every four or five days the
tribe would surround me, and ask whether I intended
going up or down the creek. At last I made them
understand that if they went up I should go up the
creek, and if they went down, I should also go
down ; and from this time they seemed to look upon
me as one of themselves, and supplied me with fish
and nardoo regularly. They were very anxious, however, to know where Burke lay, and one day when we
were fishing in the water-holes close by, I took them
to the spot. On seeing the remains, the whole party
wept bitterly, and covered them with bushes. After
this they were much kinder to me than before, and I
always told them that the white men would be here
before two moons ; and in the evening, when they
came with nardoo and fish, they used to talk about
the 'white fellows' coming, at the same time pointing
to the moon. I also told them they would receive
many presents, and they constantly asked me for
tomahawks, called by them 'bomay ho.' From this
time to when the relief-party arrived, a period of
about a month, they treated me with uniform kindness, and looked upon me as one of themselves. The
day on which I was released, one of the tribe who
had been fishing came and told me that the 'white

fellows' were coming, and the whole of the tribe who were then in camp sallied out in every direction to meet the party, while the man who brought the news took me over the creek, where I shortly saw the party coming down."

NARDOO PLANT.

CHAPTER IV.

SEARCH PARTIES AND CONCLUSION.

WE must now turn back to the time when Wright reached the Darling. As soon as it was known that Burke and the advance party had not been heard of for five months after leaving Cooper's Creek, great consternation was felt throughout all the colonies, and relief parties were organised and equipped with praiseworthy alacrity. A small contingent, under Mr. A. W. Howitt, was furnished by the Royal Society of Victoria, and started from Melbourne early in July to examine the banks of Cooper's Creek. On the 14th of August, McKinlay was sent out by the South Australian Government, with instructions to reach Cooper's Creek by way of Lake Torrens. Before the end of the same month, two other expeditions—one under Landsborough, and another under Walker—had set out to explore the region round about the Gulf of Carpentaria. These expeditions all prosecuted their search with eagerness, and through their instrumentality our geographical knowledge of the interior was greatly

BURYING THE BODY OF POOR WILLS

extended ; but Mr. Howitt's party was the only one that succeeded in getting facts about the fate of the explorers.

From his diary we learn that, with the assistance of Brahé, the depôt was reached on the 13th of September, and although this ill-fated place appeared to them to be still undisturbed, they succeeded in finding King on the fifteenth. He had been living with the blacks for more than two months, and now presented a melancholy appearance—wasted to a shadow, and hardly to be distinguished as a civilised being but by the remnants of clothes upon him. The poor fellow was sitting in a hut, while the natives were all gathered round, sitting on the ground and looking on with a most gratified and delighted expression.

After remaining two days to recruit King, Howitt and four of the men set off with the intention of burying the body of poor Wills. They found the corpse covered with sand and rushes just as King had left it, and when they had carefully collected the remains they interred them where they lay. Mr. Howitt showed their respect by conducting over the grave a short funeral ceremony. Afterwards the party heaped sand over the grave and laid bushes upon it, that the natives might know by their own tokens not to disturb the last repose of a fellow-being. To mark the spot the following inscription was cut on a tree close by :—

```
┌─────────────────────┐
│  W. J. WILLS.       │
│  XLV. Yos.          │
│  W N.W.             │
│  —A. H—             │
└─────────────────────┘
```

Mr. Howitt deferred his visit to Burke's remains, hoping that King would be able to accompany him thither ; but finding it would not be prudent to remove King for two or three days, he unwillingly took such directions as King could give, and started up the creek in search of the spot where Burke had died. After travelling eight miles they found his remains lying among tall plants under a clump of box-trees. The bones were entire, with the exception of the hands and feet, and the body had been removed from the spot where it first lay, and where the natives had placed branches over it, to about five paces distant. The revolver, loaded and capped, was lying close by, partly covered with leaves and earth, and corroded with rust. A grave was dug, and the remains of the brave explorer, wrapped in the Union-jack, were gently placed therein. On a box-tree at the head of the grave Mr. Howitt cut the following inscription :—

```
┌─────────────────────┐
│  R. O'H. B.         │
│  21/9/61.           │
│  A.. H.             │
└─────────────────────┘
```

The relief-party now went in search of the natives

"They found the remains under a clump of box-trees."

who had been so hospitable to the unfortunate explorers. On coming up to the blacks, Mr. Howitt displayed to their astonished gaze some of the things he intended to give them as a reward for their kindness. They examined the knife and tomahawk with great interest, but the looking-glass surprised them most. On seeing their faces reflected in it some seemed dazzled; others opened their eyes like saucers and made a rattling noise with their tongues, expressive of surprise. After a friendly palaver, Mr. Howitt gave them some sugar to taste. They made some absurd sleights-of-hand, as if in dread of being poisoned, and only pretended to eat it. They were then made to understand that the whole tribe were to come up to the camp next morning to receive the presents. On the following day, at ten o'clock, the friendly blacks appeared in a long procession, and at about a mile off commenced bawling at the top of their voices. When collected together, just below the camp, they numbered between thirty and forty, and the uproar they made was deafening. With the aid of King Mr. Howitt got them all seated round him, and then distributed the presents — tomahawks, knives, necklaces, looking-glasses, combs, etc. The blacks behaved as if they had never before experienced such happiness. The piccanninies were brought forward by their parents to have red ribbons tied round their dirty little heads. One old woman, who had been particularly kind to

King, was loaded **with presents.** Fifty pounds of sugar **was divided amongst them, and soon** found its **way to their mouths.** Every one had a share in a **Union-jack** pocket-handkerchief, which they were very **proud of.** On fifty pounds of flour being given to **them, they at once called it " white fellow** nardoo." The b!acks **were made to understand that** these things **had been given to them for having fed** King. Mr. Howitt **then took leave of the delighted fellows, and as he had now** accomplished **the object of his journey, he bent his course homewards.**

On **his arrival at Melbourne the sad story which he had to tell moved the minds and hearts** of all, **and deep grief prevailed throughout Australia.** In **Victoria the sorrow was intense, and it** was agreed that **the bodies of the two gallant explorers who** had forfeited their **lives in the nation's service should be** brought to Melbourne and **accorded a public** funeral. Mr. Howitt was sent **on the** painful mission of **bring-ing** down their **remains, and returned with them at** the close of the year 1862. **On the 21st of** January 1863 the mournful ceremony **took place.** By com-mon consent the greater **part of** the shops **in the** city were closed, although no official announcement had been **made intimating** that **the day** should **be** held sacred **to** the memory **of** Burke **and** Wills. The remains of the explorers had been **lying** in state at the Royal Society's Hall for a fortnight, and were now **placed in handsome coffins and conveyed to** the grave, which is near Sir Charles Hotham's monument. They were accompanied to their last resting-place by the leading gentlemen of the colony, and a procession which extended a distance of more than half-a-mile ; while the street pavements were densely thronged with spectators. The Very Rev. the Dean of Melbourne conducted the funeral service, after which three volleys were fired. The melancholy honours awarded to the brave explorers having been paid amid general mourning, the crowd dispersed and left the heroes in their quiet graves.

Honours of a more substantial kind were not forgotten. To the nearest relatives of Burke and Wills a large sum of money was voted by the Government, and King received a grant that enabled him to live comfortably for the rest of his life.

After the rewards had been given there was a less pleasing duty to be done. It was generally agreed that, with proper precautions, the disastrous termination of the expedition could have been avoided. The Government appointed a committee for the purpose of sifting out the truth, and its members examined every person in any way connected with the expedition. The following is a summary of their report :—That in dividing his party at Menindie, Mr. Burke acted most injudiciously. He made an error of judgment in engaging Mr. Wright, though a pressing emergency had arisen for the appointment of someone. Mr. Burke evinced more zeal than prudence in finally departing from Cooper's Creek without having secured communication with the settled districts, and also in undertaking so extended a journey with an insufficient supply of food. The conduct of Mr. Wright appears to be reprehensible in the highest degree. The exploration committee committed errors of a serious nature in not urging Mr. Wright's departure from the Darling. The conduct of Mr. Brahé in abandoning the depôt may be deserving of considerable censure; but a responsibility far beyond his expectations devolved upon him, and his powers of endurance gave way when pressed by the appeals of a sick comrade, who died shortly afterwards. Many of the calamities might have been averted, and none of his subordinates could have pleaded contradictory orders, had Mr. Burke kept a regular journal and given written instructions to his officers. The report ends thus :—"We cannot too deeply deplore the lamentable result of an expedition undertaken at so great a cost to the country ; but while we regret the absence of any systematic plan of operation on the part of the leader, we desire to express our admiration of his gallantry and daring, as well as the fidelity of his brave coadjutor, Mr. Wills, and their more fortunate and enduring associate, Mr. King ; and we would record our deep sympathy with the deplorable sufferings and untimely death of Mr. Burke and his fellow-comrades."

Two years later a monument was erected in honour

of the memory of Burke and Wills. It is a beautiful statue in bronze, based on granite. The sculptor was Mr. Charles Summers, an eminent Australian artist. The materials are also Australian—the bronze is composed of copper from Adelaide and tin from Beechworth, and the granite was taken from the Harcourt quarries. The bronze figures of Burke and Wills stand about 12 feet high, and are mounted on a granite pedestal, which is 15 feet high and 11 feet by 7 feet square at base. The attitude of the explorers is a very suitable and effective one. Wills is in an easy sitting posture, and Burke is standing erect with his right arm resting on his comrade's left shoulder. He is viewing the country towards the left, and is apparently drawing the attention of his companion to some of its particular features. Wills, with book on his knee and pencil in hand, is just about to make a note of them. The sides of the pedestals are adorned with bronze bas-reliefs, which represent :— (1) The starting of the expedition from the Royal Park, Melbourne ; (2) the return of Burke, Wills, and King to Cooper's Creek from Carpentaria ; (3) the blacks weeping over the dead body of Burke ; and (4) the finding of King by Howitt's search party.

On the 21st of April 1865 this stately monument was unveiled in the presence of vast numbers of people by Sir Charles Darling, Governor of Victoria. After the uncovering ceremony was performed, Sir

Charles Darling delivered the following address, which is condensed from the *Argus* of the 22nd of April :—

" At the conclusion of the cheering His Excellency said, 'Ladies and Gentlemen, Inhabitants of Victoria, I need not tell you that the sounds which are still reverberating are the echoes of what may be well termed a national honour to the illustrious dead. To make that honour as complete and perfect as we can, you have assembled in the vast numbers which meet the eye in every direction, and I accepted the position which I now occupy in the appointed ceremonial. On the 20th of August 1860 a gallant company, now known to all posterity as the " Burke and Wills Exploring Expedition," set forth, amidst the enthusiastic cheers of assembled thousands of their fellow-colonists, to win their way from the southern to the northern shore of the Australian continent. (Cheers.) A year had nearly passed away when the fact was entertained beyond a doubt that the victory had been nobly won, but that the leaders, in the exhausting struggle, had fallen almost in the hour of triumph. In the manner of their deaths, it seems to me that the distinguishing characteristics of each were strikingly illustrated. The calm and philosophic Wills begins his last letter to his father in these words—" These are probably the last lines you will ever get from me ; we are on the point of starvation, not so much from the absolute want of food, but from the want of nutriment in what we get;" and he concludes it with the tranquilly-expressed opinion and assurance, "I think to live about four or five days; my spirits are excellent." Two days later, probably but a few hours before his death, the last words recorded in his journal are literally a scientific dissertation upon the nutritious nature of the food—the nardoo plant—by means of which they had for some time protracted their existence. "Place," said the expiring Burke, instinctively recurring to his early military days, and, as I doubt not, with the picture of a fallen warrior upon the battle-field vivid in his imagination, 'place my weapon in my hand, and leave me unburied as I lie." Such was the fate of the men whom this day we mourn and honour. Then came the universal sorrow, the public funeral, the national provision for the living, and, lastly, this monument in memory of the dead. It cannot be said with truth that the people of Victoria have raised this monument in any boasting or vain-glorious spirit. It had its origin in a far more noble source. It is designed as the imperishable record of a deed which, not only on account of its intrinsic importance, but also of the high qualities which it developed in those who have achieved it, is justly believed to be worthy of high honour in the present generation and of future generations. (Cheers.) When, hereafter, shall be narrated the history of the sorrowful, yet successful

adventure which this statue is intended to com-
memorate, it will be forgotten, or remembered only
with regret, that there was once cavil and contention
whether a sounder judgment, or—as men who have
learned to believe that the issue of great events are
little under the control of human wisdom may prefer
to call it—a more fortunate judgment might not
have been exercised, and a broader beam from the
light of experience brought to bear both upon the
inception and the execution of the exploring enterprise. Nor should we, assembled as we are, not to
discuss the merits of the project, but to pay honour
to the memory of those who conquered the difficulties
which beset it, forget that, if it be true that amongst
those difficulties were the want of previous training
for, and special adaption to, the perilous task, so
much more were the glory and credit of the victory
enhanced. Nor will the sad tale of the fate of these
men be without its beneficial influence upon the intel-
lectual training and moral elevation of our people.
For, oft as it shall be told, and ofttimes it will be told
upon this very spot, Australian parents, pointing to
that commanding figure, shall bid their young and
aspiring sons to hold in admiration the ardent and
energetic spirit, the bold self-reliance, and the many
chivalrous qualities which combined to constitute the
manly nature of O'Hara Burke. (Cheers.) While
gazing on that more lowly and retiring form, they
may teach them to emulate the thirst for science, the

deep love of the Almighty's works in nature, the warm and filial family affections, the devotion to duty, self-control and submission of his own judgment to authority which he regarded as rightly conferred and exercised, and which, if I read the history of his brief career aright, pre-eminently marked the character and conduct of William Wills. (Cheers.) Better for themselves, and might haply have averted their melancholy end, if in Burke there had been more of that practical wisdom which we call prudence, and a larger measure of self-assertion and desire to sustain his own opinion, in the character of his unfortunate companion. Better, I have said, for themselves, but not for the cause of discovery and civilisation, for which they laid down their lives; for who can doubt that the knowledge of the country eastward of the line of the successful exploration, which has been acquired by the expeditions sent forth under the auspices of this and the sister colonies, to endeavour to solve the mystery of their fate, is immeasurably greater than could have been reasonably expected to follow for many years to come, had Burke and Wills returned to enjoy the peaceful laurels they had won? United in undying fame, all that was mortal of them now rests in the same hallowed grave. Well we know that "neither storied urn or animated bust" can "back to its mansion call the fleeting breath." "Honour's voice" cannot, indeed, "provoke the silent dust ;" if it could, well might their dust breathe again, and be eloquent to-day. But what man can do has now been done. There in the quiet cemetery will be placed the "storied urn." Here in the thronged city we have raised the "animated bust." It shall serve to unite also in honoured memory the names and effigies—the very form and semblance of these now celebrated men, whose great exploit has shed such lustre upon the records of exploration and discovery in this our age, and engrafted so large a share of interest and glory upon the earlier annals of Victoria.' "

OLD TIMES ON THE GOLD-FIELDS,

INCLUDING AN ACCOUNT OF

THE BALLARAT REBELLION.

Old Times on the Gold-Fields.

————◆————

" Gold, Gold, Gold, Gold—
  Bright and yellow, hard and cold."
                                —Tom Hood.

CHAPTER I.

THE CONVICT'S STRATAGEM.

THE earliest discoverer of gold in Australia is
unknown to fame. Probably he was one of
that class of colonists whom Barrington, the pickpocket, poet, and historian, describes in the oft-quoted
couplet :—

> " True patriots we, for be it understood,
>   We left our Country for our Country's good ;"

and who were employed on the roads of the colony
and on the selections of its settlers in doing the rough
work incidental to the opening of a new country.
For the first report of the existence of the precious
metal we are indebted to the cunning of a convict,

63

who attempted to regain his liberty by the following stratagem. It is related by Governor Hunter in his journal of Transactions in the Colonies. In August 1788, a report was current in the settlement which for some time appeared credible. It ran thus:—A convict named Dailey had discovered a piece of ground on which was a considerable quantity of yellow ore. Specimens of the stuff were examined by the Lieutenant-governor (in the temporary absence of the Governor), and found to contain several particles of gold. The convict was interrogated, and so plausible was his tale that the officials fully believed it, and doubted not that the man had discovered a valuable field. He was disinclined to make known its whereabouts until the Governor's return, when he promised to give full particulars of the discovery, provided he and a certain female prisoner should be liberated and given berths in one of the ships then on the point of sailing for England. But the Lieutenant-governor, impatient at the reservation of the convict, told him that unless the alleged discovery was substantiated the reward should be of rather a disappointing and irritating nature. Fearing punishment, the convict relaxed a little, and said that the mine was on the lower part of the harbour near the seashore, and offered to lead the officer to the place. Accordingly an officer and three or four soldiers embarked with the discoverer. He took them down the harbour and landed them near a wood which he

said was only a short distance from the mine. He
led the party into some dense scrub, and when in the
thick of it, managed to give them the slip. The
cheat then made for the camp as quickly as his legs
would take him round the bay, and got back early in
the afternoon. He at once informed the camp
officials that the officer was now in possession of the
gold-mine. Shortly afterwards he sneaked away
from the camp to a place of concealment. Meanwhile the party in the scrub waited some time for
their guide, and then spent hours in holloing and in
beating the bush for him. At length the officer
decided to return, and as the wily convict had persuaded him to send back the boat, the party were
obliged to march on foot round to the camp, where
they arrived at dusk, and learned with chagrin of the
trick played upon them. In a few days starvation
brought the convict from his lair. He was promptly
punished for his deceit, although he still asserted the
truth of his story. An officer was again sent with
him to find the mine, and this time the convict was
so frightened at the officer's threat to shoot him if he
attempted to practice another dodge, that he acknow-
ledged he knew of no mine at all. On being ques-
tioned about the ore produced, the convict confessed
he had filed down part of a yellow metal buckle,
mixed with it some gold filed off a guinea, blended
both with some earth, and made the conglomeration
hard as rock.

Colonel Munday relates that in 1823 a convict (one of an ironed gang working on the roads near Bathurst) was flogged for having in his possession a lump of rough gold, which the officer in charge imagined must have been the product of watches or trinkets stolen and melted down. Indeed, the toiling prisoners of the early days often picked up bits of gold, but as they could never find any other than the first small specimens, their claims for reward were disregarded and their alleged discoveries disbelieved. Long before the actual working of the gold-fields scientific adventurers had predicted the existence of gold formations in the mountain ranges explored by them, and geologists who had never visited Australia had expressed their conviction that the Australian Cordillera must be auriferous because of the remarkable similarity of their characteristics and those of other well-known gold-bearing regions.

EARLY DISCOVERIES IN NEW SOUTH WALES.

The honour of making the first report that was published lies with Count Strzelecki, for in 1839 he mentioned in the report of his exploration of New South Wales, under the heading "Gold," of "an auriferous sulphuret of iron, partly decomposed, yielding a very small quantity or proportion of gold, sufficient to attest its presence, insufficient to repay its extraction." At the request of the Governor, who was

afraid of the consequences of awakening the attention of the colonists and the thousands of convicts
to the presence of the alluring metal, the Count did
not at the time make public his discovery and belief.

Two years later the Rev. W. B. Clarke, an enthusiastic geologist, who for a long time had been
engaged in the laborious work of studying the
structure of Australia, found gold in the basin of the
Macquarie. He exhibited his specimens to his friends,
to the Government, and also communicated the facts
of his discovery to scientific friends in England.
Subsequent years of exploration increased his conviction as to the auriferous nature of the mountain
ranges, and at various times from 1842 to 1847 he
published declarations of the existence of gold-fields.
But no one attempted to profit by his disclosures, for
the authorities still considered it unsafe to disturb the
easily excited feelings of the dwellers in the penal
settlement. When Count Strzelecki returned to
England he took with him specimens of the rocks
which he had examined. His theories, together with
those of the Rev. W. B. Clarke, respecting the gold-
bearing nature of the Australian ranges, excited the
attention of Sir Roderick Murchison, and in 1844 this
eminent scientist described to the Royal Geographical
Society the comparison between the formation of the
Australian Cordillera and that of the Ural Mountains, which he himself had explored between the
years 1841 and 1843. He stated that although no

gold had been detected in the mountains of Australia, yet they possessed all the auriferous indications of the well-known gold-fields of Russia. In 1846 he again strongly expressed his belief in the richness of the Australian ranges, and recommended the tin miners of Cornwall who wanted employment to emigrate to New South Wales, and there to search for gold instead of tin.

In addition to the above-named discoveries others were reported to the Colonial Government ; but as it offered no inducement to a continuance of investigation, and as the discoverers either deemed it of little practical importance or lacked the public spirit necessary for a sustained effort to arouse the colonists, the " lucky finds " benefited no one but the finders themselves. A known instance of the latter is that of an old shepherd named McGregor. He excited a little temporary curiosity when, laden with " treasure trove," he travelled by the mail-coach to the metropolis. After this event subsided the gold-finder was unheard of for a long time, excepting for the rumour of his refusing a tempting offer of an enterprising jeweller as an inducement to disclose the locality of the treasure ground. But as McGregor " made money " without any other ostensible means than that of shepherding and gold-finding, his rise to wealth may be taken as an evidence of his success in the latter occupation.

Several stories can be told of these solitary seekers

of the precious metal; but the pursuit was usually deprecated by men of good standing, for they believed that on the presence of gold becoming widely known their own little world would be turned upside down. Some persons who successfully prosecuted further researches were pronounced as enemies to the colony when they dared to disclose the facts publicly.

But although the clamours of science and enterprise were silenced for the time, and gold, sent as specimens of the richness of the country, sceptically received and even said to be jewels and watches hidden by thieves and melted by bush fires, yet the fact of the existence of auriferous ground became at length so evident that the New South Wales Executive requested the English Government to send out an efficient geologist to examine the country. For this purpose Mr. Sutchbury, an eminent scientist, left England in September 1850.

HARGRAVES, THE PIONEER MINER.

While these discoveries were agitating the minds of a section of the agricultural and pastoral community, the one person who by his perseverance and intelligence initiated the practical working of the gold-fields of Australia was, like the father of Norval, tending his flocks and herds, and living quietly as a squatter near the town of Bathurst. The alternative droughts

and floods occurring between the years 1844 and
1848 ruined many Australian settlers, and forced
others to change their mode of life. Edward Hammond Hargraves was one of these latter unfortunates.
He had been remarkably prosperous before this
disastrous period, and even after it had sufficient to
clear himself from debt. The discovery of rich mines
in California about this time induced him to endeavour to regain his former fortune by searching for
gold in the valley of the Sacramento. There he
spent nearly two toilsome years seeking the precious
metal. His industry was poorly rewarded. During
summer the life at the diggings was tolerable, but in
the winter the cold was very severe, and Hargraves'
party suffered intensely. Even with every particle of
clothing they possessed heaped upon them they had
extreme difficulty in keeping the warmth in their
bodies whilst sleeping, and in addition to this there
was the danger of the tent being borne down by the
weight of snow upon it, and the risk of being rudely
aroused by the rough paw of any grisly bear that
might take it into his ursine head to leave the
surrounding forest in search of food. The rigours
of the climate, added to their bad luck, so dispirited
the party that at the close of the cold season they
separated. Hargraves, with a heavy heart and a
light pocket, made for San Francisco. All the
hopeful imaginings which had warmed his blood
when he embarked for the gold-country had now

been entirely dissipated by the grim realities of mining life.

As he journeyed downwards towards the seaport, probably whilst reflecting on the vicissitudes of life in general and of his own in particular, he was struck with the appearance of a deep gulch in the Sierras, which awakened old memories, and it dawned upon him that the features of the surrounding country were remarkably similar to those of the valleys near his old home in New South Wales. His two years' toiling had not weakened his energy nor dulled his observation, but it had made him more practical. He examined closely the formation of the surrounding gold-bearing districts, and found that the rocks and even the soil corresponded in many respects to the Blue Mountains of Australia. The many resemblances between the two places impressed him firmly with the belief in the existence of a gold-bearing region in New South Wales.

But his belief did not dissuade him from making another trial at the Californian diggings. In company with a friend he made several trips up the Sacramento, and succeeded in finding some payable ground ; but visions of the secluded valleys near his old home constantly haunted his mind, while the rumours he had heard of the finding of treasures in the recesses of the Blue Mountains vivified his imaginings and renewed his old desire of retrieving his fallen fortunes. He disclosed his thoughts to his

mate, and attempted to convince him of the gold-
bearing nature of the hills near Bathurst. But all
the dilations of Hargraves were wasted on his companion, who expatiated upon the foolishness of
forsaking substantial profits for the sake of shadowy
prospects, and pointed out to the enthusiast that the
geologists of Australia had already searched the
mountains thoroughly, and that if fortunes could
there be made by opening up a gold-field they would
have done so long before. Hargraves argued that
the object of the geologists in examining the ranges
was merely to verify scientific principles, and to
further scientific knowledge; but that to open up a
payable gold-field men of a very different stamp were
needed—namely, prospectors with a practical knowledge of the modes of extracting the gold, and with
will and capability to delve with the pick and to
wash the gold-sprinkled earth. Arguments, however, proved unavailing; therefore Hargraves left
his mate, and all alone shaped his course for New
South Wales.

Hargraves reached Sydney in January 1851. He
called on his former friends, and finding himself
unable to keep silent on the subject that was ever in
his thoughts, he related his experiences in California
and made his propositions; but they were looked
upon as visionary, and when he wished to borrow a
little money in order to carry them out, his request
was coldly received. Of all Hargraves' acquaintances

only one sympathised in any manner with his enthusiasm, and not one of them would lend any help
towards working out his schemes. Determined that
his purpose should not be frustrated, Hargraves
resolved, with manly self-reliance, on going alone to
the district that scientists had pronounced to be
auriferous. The few pounds required to buy a horse
and for the expenses on the way he obtained by
promising cent. per cent. interest on the loan, and
repayment of the whole within a few months.

Early in February he set out upon his lonely
journey. Every hour brought before him the old
familiar scenes which reminded him of his former
squatting life. Every step onward quickened his
feelings and increased his hopes of regaining fortune
by bringing him nearer to the Eldorado that was so
rich and bountiful in his imagination.

On the eleventh of the month the solitary horse-
man arrived at a small inn on the slope of the Blue
Mountains. He hinted to the lady the object of his
journey. She became interested in the handsome
and travel-stained enthusiast, and at his request
allowed her son to guide him to various creeks in the
vicinity.

Early the next morning Hargraves, accompanied
by the boy, left the inn. After a long journey
through the bush they came to Summerhill Creek.
This was the destination of our gold-fields' pioneer.
A good look around confirmed his anticipations, and

with glowing feelings he gazed at the realities of
what had haunted him in his visions.   Then, in order
to relieve the intense strain which his mind had con-
tinuously endured for the past few months, he lay
quietly down on the banks of the quiet creek.   After
a short rest, he took pick and trowel in hand, and
prospected along the water-course.   Five panfuls of
earth and gravel were in a short time collected, and
in four of them he found gold.   Much elated at this
result, and as the day was now drawing to a close, he
decided to return to the inn and renew his searches
on the morrow.

When he reached the inn he very carefully wrote
an account of his doings and discoveries during the
day, for well he knew that besides being a fortunate
one for himself, the 12th of February 1851 would be
a memorable day in the annals of Australia.

The next day he further examined the creek, and
for the two following months he continued his prospecting with unflagging industry.   His researches
were crowned with indubitable success.   He saw
enough of the precious metal to convince him of
the richness of the gold-field, and also discovered
indications of its presence in many surrounding
places.   Then, feeling satisfied that the object of
his expedition was accomplished, even beyond his
expectations, he returned to Sydney for the purpose
of obtaining a reward for his discoveries, and making
them known to the public.

The Government of New South Wales received with suspicion the discoverer's statement that he could point out a rich gold-field within the boundaries of the colony. The many pretended gold discoveries had made them chary of belief in such reports, besides which the convict element was still a cause of fear; while, above all, it was thought that the existence of genuine gold-fields in the Blue Mountains would long since have been discovered and made known by the many geologists and other scientists who had explored the ranges.

But Hargraves was too sensible a man to be discouraged by the rebuffs of a Conservative Government. He saw the importance of his discovery, and by dint of personally interviewing the Colonial Secretary, he drew from that gentleman a recognition of it; and with characteristic caution and shrewdness obtained a guarantee of the Government reward in the event of its proving valuable. Then he undertook to disclose the secret to the Government geologist, and also persuaded persons to accompany him to the scene of his discoveries. The latter he accomplished by delivering a lecture at the town of Bathurst, and by forming companies of miners, to whom he took upon himself to give a Government authority to dig for the precious metal. The excitement raised in the town spread through the surrounding districts, and very soon numbers of shepherds were allured from the green pastures unto the "yellow sands."

This rushing away from the ordinary employments was expected to entail great losses to the stock-holders, while it was feared by the more timid that the scenes once enacted at the Californian diggings would soon be acted over again on these fields.

The Government geologist was in due time de-spatched to test the value and importance of the alleged discoveries. He fully confirmed the truth of the statements made by Hargraves, and advised the Government to engage the pioneer to carry out their measures, because the experience and knowledge in mining matters which he had acquired in California would make him specially valuable at the time of the opening up of fresh diggings.

Before the end of May, one thousand men were on the spot selected by Hargraves, and the extent and rich productiveness of the gold-fields had become so widely known that hundreds flocked daily out of Sydney. The Government, after some vain efforts to check this rush, wisely desisted from the attempt, and proceeded to establish regulations to preserve good order at the diggings. They issued licenses, without which it was illegal to dig or search for gold, and also enforced, with the aid of a body of foot and mounted police, obedience to the laws.

Hargraves was appointed a Commissioner of Crown Lands for the purpose of searching, on behalf of the Government, for further fields of employment for gold-diggers. In addition to his salary as

A Bush Fire.

Commissioner, he was at once rewarded £500 for his valuable discoveries ; and subsequently, when the magnitude of their importance had become more generally realised, this amount was increased by grants from the New South Wales and Victorian Governments, and by testimonials from the citizens of Sydney and Melbourne, to the handsome extent of £15,000.

Edward Hammond Hargraves was presented to the Queen in 1853 as the Australian gold discoverer. The liberal rewards and honours bestowed upon him are but an infinitesimal portion of the wealth and fame which have accrued to the colonists through his discovery. And it is mainly owing to the thoughtfulness, cleverness, and enterprising perseverance of Hargraves, that in an extremely short period Australia has taken an advanced position among the nations of the world.

THE ABORIGINAL DISCOVERER.

The excitement which Hargraves' revelations had raised abated a little early in June, for the weather was cold, wet, and inclement, and the digger's life was thus rendered miserable. The rains flooded the creeks and drenched the diggers, the floods effectively preventing all from gold-hunting. Many on the gold-fields became disheartened, and returned to Sydney with such gloomy reports that for a time the rush from town was wholly checked. Towards the close of June, however, a shepherd picked up gold in the neighbourhood of Turon river. News of this rapidly spread round the district, and in a few days hundreds were on the spot hunting greedily for further treasures.

The next "lucky find" was a magnificent one. Near the scene of this new rush an aboriginal, obtaining a brief respite from minding his master's sheep, took a tomahawk in hand and amused himself by playing the geologist. He wandered about chipping the rocks and examining the country adjacent to the sheep run. A glittering, yellow substance sticking out of a rock attracted his attention. Applying his tomahawk, he struck off a portion, when a lump of the metal so coveted by the white fellow was revealed to his delighted gaze. The intelligent black darted away to bring his master to behold the golden prize. Shortly afterwards he and his master (Dr. Kerr) arrived at the spot. By working laboriously with a sledge-hammer, and breaking the gigantic mass into three pieces, they managed to disembowel quartz and gold weighing over two hundredweight. Out of these lumps the mammoth treasure-trove of one hundred and sixty pounds of pure gold was obtained, which on being sold realised the magnificent sum of £4160.

This "Kerr Hundredweight" eclipsed anything ever previously seen in the shape of nuggets. The rumour of its dazzling proportions attracted the notice of adventurers, and increased tenfold the stream of fortune-hunters that flowed towards the Turon mines. The district soon became so prosperous, and the price of land in the vicinity so high, that land-holders in other districts, fearing a depreciation in the value of their property, were induced to offer rewards for discoveries in their own neighbourhood.

But the fame of the New South Wales gold-fields was short-lived, for greater treasures were a few months afterwards discovered in Victoria ; and the continued steady yield there put all other discoveries completely in the shade. The shifting population of the original diggings at once withdrew from the tributaries of the Macquarie, and numbers on their way thither deflected their course on hearing of the richer auriferous creeks in the neighbouring colony.

CHAPTER II.

"Gold, precious yellow, glittering gold !
What can it not do and undo ?"

THE exodus of gold-seekers from the Port Philip
district to the Sydney side alarmed its leading men, for they were aware of the necessity of
an increasing population in a rising pastoral community such as theirs. The agricultural and pastoral
interests were likely to be seriously affected if the
bone and sinew of the labourers sought employment
in the rich mines on the banks of the Turon instead
of on the corn-fields and pasture lands of the Port
Philip district. Besides, the Port Philippians had
for some time been endeavouring to procure separation from New South Wales ; in fact, the act of
separation was just about to take place, and this
stroke of luck in favour of the older colony by
heightening its prospects correspondingly humbled
those of the new colony, and tended to sink it into
insignificance. The Mayor of Melbourne, therefore,
convened a public meeting, at which several energetic

and influential men were formed into a Gold Discovery Committee. This committee, in order to avert the threatened crisis, offered a reward of two hundred guineas to the person who should discover a payable gold-field within the district.

JAMES ESMOND, THE VICTORIAN PIONEER DIGGER.

About a month after this meeting in Melbourne the Geelong newspapers announced the discovery of gold at Clunes, on the 1st of July, by James Esmond, a pioneer who does not appear to have heard of the promised reward.

The adventures of this first of Victorian diggers were in many respects similar to those of Hargraves. In 1848 James Esmond was driver of the mail-coach between Buninyong and Horsham. For several years he had filled the box-seat, in which position he received commendation for his careful handling of the horses, and his courteous behaviour to his passengers. But at length the dreary monotony of his long and lonely route through the bush and over the rocky ranges of the Pyrenees proved too wearisome for the roving disposition of the young driver. He therefore threw down the reins and abandoned his mail contract. Glowing reports of the golden treasures of California were being circulated throughout the district, and were listened to with eager ears by young Esmond. He would gratify an intense love of adventure that prompted him to go to the diggings, and at the same time woo Dame Fortune and win her golden smiles. Thus he determined, and in due course arrived in California. He soon experienced the discomforts of a digger's life, but found very little gold. Ill-luck attended all his toiling, and made him so thoroughly disgusted with digging life that he resolved to return to his old occupation, which, although lacking the excitement of gold-hunting, was also without its bitter discouragement and uncertainty. Esmond returned to Sydney on the ship that brought Hargraves back to New South Wales. This was purely by chance, and probably the two men scarcely ever spoke to each other during the voyage. After two months spent idly in Sydney he came on to Melbourne in a very slow sailing vessel, which took three weeks to make the short voyage between the two capitals. Esmond journeyed to Buninyong, and as his old position was occupied by another man, he was obliged to take to another calling. Nothing better than bushman's work could be had, so he undertook to cut down timber and build log-huts on a station in the Pyrenees. This arduous work was shared by one companion. In its loneliness and want of variety it was so directly opposite to the eventfulness of Esmond's last occupation that the two men might work for weeks without seeing another human being. But the dull uniformity of the lives of the two men was suddenly changed by the arrival on the scene of a German geologist named Dr. Bruhn, who showed to Esmond and his mate rich specimens of gold found in the neighbourhood, and told the wondering pair that a practical miner might easily discover a payable gold-field in the district. This unexpected announcement immediately filled Esmond with the desire to once again tempt Dame Fortune. He easily persuaded his mate to join him in the adventure, and the pair discontinued tree-felling and hut-building, and with pick and tin-dish set forth in search of fortune's golden gifts. As an early poetical chronicler thus puts it :—

> " Behold him, along with his partner, set out
> To prospect the unexplor'd ranges about ;
> They pass the poor natives, crouch'd round their rude fire,
> Nor linger the beautiful birds to admire.
> The kangaroo furtively peeps from its lair,
> The cunning opossum bestows a wild stare ;
> But till they find gold little rest will they draw."

Esmond and his companion began their prospecting tour on the 1st of July 1851 (separation day). They soon attained the object of their expedition, and with very little effort. On reaching the banks of Deep Creek, a tributary of the Loddon, they were gladdened by the sight of glistening quartz. A little diligent fossicking there was rewarded by the unearthing of a few rich specimens of grain gold, or what appeared to be such. In order to make sure of the richness of the metal, Esmond determined to have the specimen tested by an assayer at Geelong. On arriving at that town the pureness of the gold was vouched for, and eager inquiries were made for the locality where the precious treasure could be found.

Esmond declined to divulge his secret, and hastened to obtain the necessary implements and utensils for working the coveted field. It was the 6th of July before his digging expedition (the first in Victoria), which consisted of three men besides himself, was fully equipped. Before leaving Geelong, Esmond disclosed his destination to the assayer, who advised other parties fitting out for the Turon diggings to remain in the district, because of the probability of richer gold-fields being shortly found close at hand.

In the meantime another discovery was announced. A party of six men found sprinklings of gold in the bed of Anderson's Creek, a tributary of the Yarra, and only a few miles from Melbourne. These discoveries were effective in stemming the tide of emigration to New South Wales. Esmond's field attracted about thirty men, and produced satisfactory results until the end of August. It then became evident that the precious yellow grains were no longer to be found in the alluvial deposits. The men at Clunes were getting into severe straits because of the poorness of the shallow diggings, when a visitor to the place brought the welcome news of fresh discoveries and encouraging prospects for diggers in the neighbourhood of Buninyong.

Amongst the first to leave the Clunes diggings was Esmond, its original prospector. He joined a party of nine, who marched over the hills to the newly-discovered fields. With this party we will leave the pioneer, for he afterwards worked in company with others, and met with no extraordinary adventures. Though remarkably successful as a digger, he was singularly unfortunate in his speculations. Subsequently £1000 was voted to him in reward for his discoveries. He also received a grant of a piece of land on the site of the first gold-field.

OTHER PIONEERS.

The rich discoveries at Clunes excited the cupidity, or perhaps we should say the spirit of adventure, of many of the colonists, and tempted them to leave their ordinary occupations to join in the search for gold. A resident of Buninyong, named Thomas Hiscock, was induced to examine the surrounding hills. A brief search was rewarded by the discovery, in one of the many gullies that wind among the hills, of some bright yellow grains, which, from their weight and lustre, he thought must be the precious metal he was in quest of. These specimens he took to Geelong for the purpose of having them tested by a competent assayer. He arrived at Geelong on the 10th of August, and had some difficulty in finding a reliable gold expert ; but a gentleman who had seen Esmond's specimens a few weeks before pronounced Hiscock's "find" to be true gold, and much finer and more glistening than that found at Clunes. When Hiscock's discovery was made public a number of workmen and idlers left Geelong and set out for the gully. But the weather was cold, and the continual pouring of rain damped the ardour of most of the adventurers ere they began to seek for the precious metal. Many remained in the township of Buninyong, not venturing to camp on the hills, because the ground there was so muddy and the gully so slushy as to render living under canvas extremely miserable, and fossicking for gold almost impossible. Despite these drawbacks there were within a fortnight of the arrival of its discoverer in Geelong over forty diggers at work in Hiscock's gully. But ill-luck attended the efforts of most of these pioneers, and continual disappointments forced many of them to try the diggings at Clunes.

With this object in view, a digger named **Dunlop** packed up his tent and baggage, and would have taken himself to Clunes ; but when he learned that four pounds was the price of carriage in the waggon about to start for that place, he resolved to give

Buninyong another trial. Early next morning he disappeared from the township. In the evening he returned to his wondering mate and showed him a match-box containing half an ounce of gold, which he said was the result of that day's seeking amongst the hills five or six miles away. His mate would not believe his tale, but at break of day Dunlop again disappeared—this time in company with a friend named Regan. A few days elapsed, and the two men being still away, his mate went out in search of them. Then the absence of the three men was remarked at the hotel where they had been lodging. Four other men, suspecting the cause of the sudden disappearance, and hoping to share in any fresh discoveries, went stealthily out of the township and endeavoured to track the supposed lucky prospectors. But the latter did not wish to be discovered, and attempted to elude their pursuers. However, all their efforts to escape observation were in vain, for in a very short time the place that Dunlop had discovered attracted almost all the diggers from Buninyong, who soon displaced the few miserable native wanderers who had roamed over Poverty Flat—as it was gruesomely named—"monarchs of all they surveyed, and lords of the fowl and the brute."

Shortly afterwards the treasures of Golden Point were revealed. A family named Cavanagh had secured a half-worked claim, and having carried it below a layer of pipe-clay into the midst of some decayed slate, they struck the first of those rich pockets which were afterwards found in such abundance throughout the Golden Point Field.

Before the end of August the mineral richness of the neighbouring creeks became evident, and numbers of nimble fossickers gathered the first crops of the Ballarat gold-fields. In September rich diggings were opened at Mount Alexander, and two or three weeks later the yield of those at Bendigo eclipsed for a time the glories of all other fields.

CHAPTER III.

EFFECT OF DISCOVERIES.

" Like stragglers from an army, orderless,
　The adventurers toward their haven press ;
　Their ardent minds, ignoring present care,
　Imagine future "lobs" of which they share.
　Through their hot brains what splendid visions speed
　Of golden *claims* directly on the *lead*,
　Enabling them thro' hoary Age to sail
　With hawsers moored to Competence's tail !

　　.　　.　　.　　.　　.　　.　　.

　How chang'd the landscape since the paleface came,
　How hard to recognise it as the same !
　The earth no longer wears her garb of green,
　But grave-like holes may everywhere be seen ;
　The forest fell'd to cook the miners' food,
　The sadden'd Natives scatter'd and subdu'd."

　　　　　　　The New Rush.—J. RODGERS.

THE wonderful effect of the valuable discoveries made during the first few months of gold-seeking soon became apparent in Melbourne and Geelong, owing to the rapid departure for the diggings of great numbers of the townsfolks, who abandoned their ordinary vocations in order to get a share of the profuse rewards there meted out by Mother Earth to the industrious or the lucky.

The Victorian population at this time was only 77,000, of which 30,000 were concentrated in the two principal towns. Nearly all these people became mad for gold. The whole of the colony was stirred to its inmost depths, and underwent a total revolution in all its social relations.

Almost the first manifestation of the change was shown in the sudden appearance of an immense motley throng upon the roads that converged to the gold-fields. Thousands of men of every walk in life —rich and poor, old and young, sturdy and weak— were enticed from the comforts and delights of the domestic hearth, and from the conveniences and amusements of town life, by the allurements of the glittering prizes which Dame Fortune was lavishly dealing out to the pioneer prospectors, and which seemed to dangle before the expectant eyes of every-one. What a strange and entertaining sight the thickly-thronged roads must have presented to the observant student of human nature! Many a tramp hopefully toiling along with swag on back ; bands of mechanics with lumbering drays and bony nags to assist in transporting the heavy necessaries ; parties with light hand-carts and wheel-barrows energetically pushing and pulling their primitive vehicles; shopmen in spring carts ; doctors and lawyers in first-class

THE RUSH TO THE DIGGINGS.

gigs and buggies. The whole of these, from beggar to barrister, from pickpocket to parson, were to be seen hieing along dusty roads and journeying through hitherto untrodden forest, all impelled by the one covetous desire to the one end—the gold-fields, where, perchance, they might reap a golden harvest without the laborious years of working and the wearisomeness of waiting, which are the usual checks to success in other pursuits.

Ere these fortune-hunters reached the Eldorado of their wishes, many obstacles had to be overcome. The roughness of the road, the yielding nature of the bush tracks, and general unevenness of the ground, occasioned many a poor horse to knock under and leave his master or masters in a sorry plight. Their fellow-wayfarers seeing such a predicament would sometimes lend a helping hand; and it was not uncommon to see thirty or forty men dragging a dray up some of the steep hills by means of ropes, or carrying on their backs portions of a heavy load.

A number of the travellers were free and independent. These, carrying all their property with them, usually made a day's journey of about twenty miles; then, after an *al-fresco* meal, they lay down in the open-air, with their blankets wrapped like martial cloaks around them, and were lulled to sleep by the breezy murmurs of the wild bush. Others, ignorant of the obstacles they had to encounter, rushed away from town insufficiently

8

supplied with provisions, and the few public-houses on the way became quickly packed to confusion by these half-famished wanderers, demanding food and drink.

Many of the first arrivals on the fields soon found out that the life of a digger was not all honey, and, after a few bitter experiences, either went back to their old employments in the town, or adapted themselves to the requirements of the new order of things by supplying the diggers' camp with provisions —an occupation which was generally quite as lucrative as that of the average digger. Meanwhile, the fame of the Victorian gold-fields had circulated throughout the adjacent colonies. Very soon the tide of emigration was turned from the Turon mines, and flowed in the direction of Ballarat and its vicinity. It poured into the auriferous creeks in the shape of an immense living mass, every unit big with expectation, and bent on ferreting out and appropriating some fragment of the golden lodestone.

The bush surrounding the diggings was quickly thinned of its timber—its red gum, stringy bark, and box trees serving as good fuel for the culinary fire of the digger. Even the tallest and most massive giants of the forest were not spared, and soon the scene was completely shorn of its pristine sylvan beauty. Verdant hillocks and grassy mounds, which in primeval days had been the peaceful browsing and grazing grounds of the kangaroo and its species, and the happy hunting grounds of their scarcely human enemy, the aboriginal black, were speedily changed into yellow-coloured upheavals, which from a distance presented to the interested spectator the lively appearance of great ant-hills warming with busy workers, who now dropped into pits cut in the slopes, and anon reappeared bearing heavy loads, with which they impetuously rushed to the turbid waters of the nearest gully.

On the diggings everyone was subjected to the sway of the golden metal, and the effect of the spell on the different temperaments was as interesting as they were varied. In some of the diggers the sympathetic springs of life's action seemed to be completely clogged ; the demon of avarice held complete dominion, and rendered these men forgetful of the commonest offices of humanity. But over others the spell was not so potent, or its sordid effect so marked—an occasional pausing or ceasing from work in order to exchange civilities, or to do a friendly action, betokening that a desire for the amenities of life was not entirely obliterated even among the rough hairy diggers in their most cupiditative pursuit.

A year later the fame of the enormous yield of the Victorian gold-fields had astonished the whole world, and quickly attracted numerous ship-loads of emigrants from every centre of civilisation. This great influx set in about September 1852, and

doubled the population before the end of the year.
During 1852 and 1853 Victoria became the most
populous of the colonies by the arrival of nearly
200,000 persons, the arrivals in Hobson's Bay
averaging about 1800 weekly.

Many of the more sober-minded of the colonists
were greatly concerned in mind by this tremendous
inundation; but the go-ahead or hopefully-inclined
trusted that the great successive waves of fresh
inhabitants from the thickly-populated portions of
the old world would be the making of the colony.
The influx was certainly an immediate boon to the
sheep-farmers of the period. The state of the colony
in the early days was well described by London
Punch in the lines—

> "The land of the South that lies under our feet,
> Deficient in mouths, over-burdened with meat."

But now the order of things was reversed, and, owing
to the ever-increasing number of mouths to be fed,
the prices of all articles of consumption went up
enormously.

CANVAS TOWN.

House accommodation became wholly inadequate
to meet the requirements of the great multitude, and
holders of tenements made enormous profits by
letting portions of their mean dwellings at extraordinary high rents. Many respectable and **even**

monied persons were obliged to live in tents, while
large numbers passed both day and night with no
other roof than the blue sky overhead.

A unique suburb sprang into existence on the
south side of the Yarra. It was improvised by the
surplus population who could not obtain shelter in
over-crowded Melbourne. Its name—Canvas Town
—describes its construction. It was pleasantly situ-
ated, commencing on a grassy slope, and was laid
out in streets and lanes ; the principal thoroughfares
being crowded with boarding-houses and shops, all
of canvas. The Government charged the occupant
of each impromptu dwelling five shillings per week
for the right to camp on the site. All sorts of people
mingled together in this primitive township, and
many new chums here took their first lessons in
roughing it.

RAG FAIR.

Another novel and interesting scene was the
market which sprang into existence on the wharf
where most of the arrivals landed. The exorbitant
rates charged for cart-hire and store-rent precluded
many from removing their heavy luggage, which
remained day after day piled up in huge heaps by
the water-side. At length some of the emigrants
devised a plan for its sale. An impromptu bazaar
was opened ; the sea-chests were placed back to
back, and arrayed in lines with the up-turned lids

strewed with the contents, so that the merchandise was fully exposed for inspection. A brisk trade soon sprang up, in which abundance of wearing apparel and household furniture was sold at "alarming sacrifices," as the exigencies of the times demanded the immediate disposal of all cumbrous articles. The low prices increased the popularity of this "Rag Fair," as it was called, and the business became at last so considerable that, in response to the complaints of shopkeepers, the City Council issued an order for its stoppage.

In striking contrast to the efforts made by these new chums in getting rid of their superfluities in order to buy a suitable outfit for the diggings, were the dissipations and freaks of many returned diggers, who, having been lucky on the gold-fields, were now recklessly squandering their quickly-acquired wealth. These extravagant displays tended to quicken the movements of new arrivals in their preparations, and to keep up a constant flowing of the population between the rich diggings and the town.

NEW CHUMS AND OLD CHUMS.

The picturesqueness of life on the gold-fields was heightened by the appearance on the scene of the immigrants, who brought with them the many peculiarities of their national traits. The bluff Englishman and the mirthful Irishman, the cautious

Scotchman and the volatile Frenchman, the industrious German and the 'cute Yankee—all could be seen working in close proximity ; while the indefatigable Chinaman toiling close at hand, generally in claims abandoned by his more robust European neighbours, added not a little to the varied attraction of the scene.

These representatives of different nationalities brought with them their own distinctive notions of rights and freedom ; but their common occupation and necessary intercourse modified many objectionable peculiarities. Differences of class, too, were laid aside ; the illiterate labourer ranked on the same footing as the scholarly adventurer, provided they both possessed a strong arm and a stout heart. In short, the motley throng on the gold-field formed a vast republic of labour.

The general greeting to men of aristocratic birth or manners was superciliously conveyed by the title of " swell," "genteel cove," or the slang term " Joe." These gentlemen-diggers being mostly unfit for roughing it, were sometimes engaged by the lords of labour to light the fires and wash tin-plates and pannikins. Of course this reversion of the usual order of things had an inflatory effect on the common labourers, whose superior bone and sinew made them for the time the better men. As an instance of it, we quote from McCombie :—

" A squatter had come to the diggings to hire

shearers, and seeing a party of men who seemed to be idle, he asked if they would engage for the sheep-shearing. After a little hesitation one of the party replied that they would if they had their own terms. On being asked to state them, he replied, in a bantering tone, *the wool upon their backs.* The squatter turned away, but was soon recalled. He quickly obeyed the summons, supposing the men had thought better of his offer. The spokes-man of the party now told, with a knowing leer, that his mates and himself were in want of a *cook*, and they had come to the resolution to offer him a pound a day if he would condescend to accept the office."

Again, the appearance of anything like fine manners or " swell " clothes was instantly reprobated. Innocent offenders in these respects were quickly reminded of the incongruity between Continental and Victorian ceremonies and fashions. New chums frequently presented themselves on the diggings clothed in London or Paris costumes, and thus advertised, they were welcomed with noisy merri-ment, and at once named " Joeys " amidst ironical cheers. An anecdote of this nature follows ; it is extracted from *Glimpses of Life in Victoria* :—

" A very pleasant, gentlemanly young fellow, lately arrived, and inexperienced in the customs of the colony, ventured one day among the diggings wearing the conspicuous tall hat which he had always been used to wear at home. He was instantly assailed by cries of 'Joe! Joe!' which were re-echoed on every side and reiterated by hundreds of voices, as one man after another popped up his head from the hole in which he was working and joined in the mocking chorus. Quite unconscious that he was the observed of all eyes, he walked unsuspectingly on, but the clamour still increased, and many a finger pointed at him at length caused him to guess pretty correctly the cause of the commotion. He had much ready wit and self-possession, and did not deliberate long on the course to pursue, but taking off his hat he turned from side to side and made a series of profound bows to the noisy community. The effect was all that he could have desired, for the piercing shouts were presently exchanged for a hearty cheer, and he was suffered to continue his way unmolested."

From what has been said it may be gathered that in the early muscular days of the colony work made the man, and want of it the fellow. The feeble-bodied digger was nowhere in the race for wealth, and many a solitary sickly one dropped out of existence unknown to any of his friends, and not even missed in the ever-varying excitements of the times.

CHAPTER IV.

SLY GROG SHANTIES.

"The diggings hoh ! the diggings hah !
Shout for the diggings, shout hurrah !"
— *Diggers' Chorus.*

DURING the hours of relaxation the proceedings on the diggings contrasted vividly with the day's employment. The end of the day's labours was in the early days announced by the firing of a gun from the tent of the Commissioner. Then followed a general abandonment of the chip, chip of the pick against the rock, the delving in the mud, the barrow-wheeling, the cradle-rocking, and the puddling in clayey water-holes. With mud-bespattered shirt, clay-soiled pants, and heavy yellow-stained boots, each digging-party sought its tent. Then the ringing sound of axes wielded by brawny arms told of preparations for the evening meal. Hundreds of thin lines of blue smoke ascending from as many fires joined to make the large volume that wafted overhead. Soon the singing of the kettles on the

ON THE GOLD FIELDS.

blazing logs cheered the weary digger with the prospect of a fragrant pannikin of tea to moisten his damper—a somewhat heavy staff of life, but one admirably adapted to support the toiling gold-seeker.

Refreshed and stimulated by the evening meal, the diggers would then light their pipes, and soon the curling wreaths of smoke circling round betokened the complacency of the different companies. Then yarns were spun, arguments held, and songs sung, until the loquacious and musical ones became exhausted or the listeners had fallen asleep.

SLY GROG SHANTIES.

But the harmony of such scenes was but too often disturbed by the noise of drunken revelry—

> " Sottish sets more opulent than wise,
> The sly grog shanties and hotel comprise ;
> Wasting the profits of their jewell'd claims,
> In hurtful stimulants and risky games."

Although selling intoxicating liquors was an illegal offence on the first gold-fields, yet, despite the vigilance of the Commissioners, the votaries of Bacchus were supplied with their spirituous comforts by certain storekeepers, who cunningly contrived to conceal the illicit decoctions and carry on a brisk trade on the sly.

The ingenuity of these sly grog-sellers in baffling the police evoked a corresponding sharpness on the part of the Commissioners in detecting illegal practices. When a plant was discovered its contents were either confiscated or wasted, and its owner, if found, was visited with the full wrath of the authorities, and afterwards punished according to the law.

An instance of the summary manner in which some cases were dealt with is here inserted from *Glimpses of Life in Victoria :—*

" We stopped next before an empty tent of ample dimensions, which appeared to court the light of day, for it was half-open, and its interior was unusually neat and clean. A heap of digging implements lay in front, and a pair of moleskin trousers were hung artlessly over the top of the tent (Mr. ——'s informant had bidden him to take notice of a tent so decorated). Inside, at the furthest end, stood a large-sized bedstead, white and clean to outward appearance, with a deep valance running round the foot. Nothing in the least suspicious was visible in this neat open dwelling ; nevertheless, it was to the pure white couch that Mr. ——, having dismounted, marched straight up through the opening of the tent, with the order that it should be searched forthwith. The valance was lifted and disclosed a large quarter cask and several kegs full of rum, which were taken up and deposited outside. 'Who is the owner of this tent?' demanded Mr. —— again of the crowd which had gathered around him. The question was repeated, but it fell, as before, on a silent assembly.

" 'Since this property has no owner,' said he, 'I will quickly show you what I will do with it.'

" Catching hold of a pick that was lying at hand, he set to work himself to remove the top of the cask, then dipping a bucket into the liquor, he soused the tent inside and out ; the kegs were emptied out in like manner, till the whole of the hoarded store was spilt, and the air was reeking with the smell of rum. Then striking a match, he applied it to the ground, and the spirit igniting set fire to the tent, which flared and blazed up in a moment, throwing a ruddy glow over the throng of angry faces that looked on in gloomy silence, broken only by a half-smothered imprecation from some of the most daring of the crowd. The flames arose higher and higher, when suddenly a gun went off, producing for the moment an effect which might truly be called sensational. No one knew whence the discharge had come, whether some hand in the angry crowd had fired it, and whether others might follow ; presently, however, it was ascertained that the gun had been in the tent, and that the fire had caused it to explode. 'We had better move off,' said a voice ; 'there might be more guns yet in that tent.'

" As might be expected, such proceedings were viewed by a certain class of diggers with anything but satisfaction. Cries of 'It's a —— shame,' and 'Don't waste the —— grog,' evinced the boiling feelings of the rougher element. Even the lovers of order were generally mortified by the restrictions of the liquor laws."

CHAPTER V.

THE DIGGER'S LICENSE.

"Let active laws apply the needful curb,
   To guard the peace that riot would disturb;
And Liberty, preserved from wild excess,
   Shall raise no feuds for armies to suppress."

                —COWPER.

ANOTHER and greater grievance which daily stirred up strife between the diggers and the Commissioners was the gold-digger's license. The collecting of the license fee was from the first an invidious duty, which demanded a vast deal of tact on the part of the Commissioners and staff, for the diggers were always opposed to the tax, and many were the ruses they adopted to escape its payment.

The first skirmish in connection with this impost took place at the Golden Point, Ballarat. The diggers at the Point understood that no tax would be charged for the month of September 1852, as the Government wished to encourage prospecting on new gold-fields. But the Commissioners, on arriving at Golden Point, perceived by the general appearance of cheerfulness that the field was yielding good returns.

9

Yet the diggers gave most evasive answers to their
inquiries as to the result of the prospecting, and
reminded them that the Government would forego
the September tax. These artifices led the Commissioners to suspect that the men on the Point were
more than ordinarily successful, and were planting
their gains out of the range of the official eye. But
an old pioneer named Connor failed to hide a
pannikin full of gold dust, and its discovery con-
firming the suspicions of the Commissioners, they
concluded that the community was prosperous
enough to pay the tax, and thereupon announced
that a license fee of fifteen shillings must be paid for
the latter half of the month.

This proclamation aroused the indignation of the
diggers. They held a meeting, at which a man
named Swindells mounted the "stump," and de-
nounced the sharp conduct of the officials. A
deputation of two (the orator and a Mr. Oddie)
were appointed to interview the Commissioners, in
order to get them to revoke their decision. This the
Commissioners bluntly refused to do, and the two
representatives, after a wordy war, were compelled to
retreat. The diggers now became exasperated, and
when they further heard that Connor, the man whose
carelessness was the immediate cause of the levying
of the tax, had actually paid it, their wrath knew no
bounds. They bonnetted him, pelted him with mud
till he was almost covered, and would have proceeded

to greater indignities had not Oddie and a few others curbed their unbridled feelings by referring to the grey hairs of the delinquent.

Notwithstanding this heated manifestation of ill-temper, the Commissioners enforced the license fee, and it was noticed, as is very often the case in popular demonstrations, that many of the most violent of the diggers succumbed the readiest under official pressure. But the last to give in was Swindells, so that when he did apply for a license his consistent obnoxiousness was remembered by the Commissioners to his disadvantage, and they refused to grant him one.

To recompense him the diggers, therefore, subscribed and presented him with 12 ounces of gold for his efforts on their behalf. Swindells afterwards went to Forest Creek diggings, and as a report came to the Point that a license was again denied him, the diggers asserted that the Government had determined to put a stop to his mining in Victoria because he had championed their cause at Ballarat.

On first hearing of the gold discoveries the Executive of Victoria had exercised their prerogative, as representatives of the Crown, to claim all precious metals found within the colony. A notice was issued forbidding anyone to dig for gold unless under certain rules, one of which was that the gold-seeker should pay a license fee of 30s. per month before commencing his search.

The colony, which was then in its infancy, was
governed according to the Crown Colony system;
but by the incessant arrivals its population so
increased in numerical strength as to be almost
beyond the control of the ruling powers. The
Government appear to have been particularly puzzled
as to their duties towards the vast irregular society
upon the gold-fields. That it should be regarded as
merely a migratory flight of population from the old
centres of civilisation, which having swooped down
upon the gold sown broadcast in the land, would
presently return whither it came, carrying away the
best of the gold harvest, was the idea which must
have occupied the minds of the authorities, for they
never attempted to make the gold-fields' population
a part of the colony until the clamouring of the
insurrectionists at Ballarat dispelled the illusion, and
apprised them of the impolicy of delay in according
a social status to the gold-digger.

The Executive of the day sought to solve the
difficulty by the appointment of Police Magistrates
or Commissioners, whose chief duty seems to have
been the enforcement of the gold-tax act.

Now in the digging community were many factious
adventurers, whose peculiar ideas of rights and
liberties would have clashed with any form of
government. These malcontents exasperated the
Commissioners, and caused the power lodged in them
to be used in its fullest extent. The police force

were directed to keep continual watch on the fields, and compel the production of licenses as often as they pleased to ask for them. Even the prudent exercise of this authority would no doubt have been galling to law-abiding miners, for tax-paying, without the surveillance, is not as a rule congenial to the feelings of members of settled communities.

But the majority of the police officers were generally overbearing and insolent, and their want of tact when dealing with the rough natures on the diggings greatly increased the embarrassment of affairs. A license-hunt was the name among the diggers for the collecting of the tax—the police being the hounds, while many a digger in his wily attempt to escape payment proved himself a veritable fox in cunning.

DIGGER-HUNTING ANECDOTES.

The following vigorous descriptions of this tax-collecting graphically portray the feelings of both diggers and officials. The first is extracted from Kelly's entertaining *Life in Victoria* :—

" W——n shouted down, ' Come up, boys—come along, quick; the game is started !' and as I was being hoisted up I heard the swelling uproar and the loud chorus of ' Joes' from every side. As I gained the surface everybody was in commotion—diggers with their licenses lowering down their mates without them; others, with folded arms, cursing the system and damning the Government; some stealing away like hares when hounds are in the neighbourhood; and several 'tally-ho'd,' bursting from points where they could escape arrest, while 'Joe! Joe! Joe! Joe! Joe! Joe!' resounded on all sides; the half-clad Amazons running up the hill-sides, like so many bearers of the 'fiery cross,' to spread to the neighbouring gullies the commencement of the police foray. The police, acting on a preconcerted plan of attack, kept closing in upon their prey; the mounted portion, under the commander-in-chief, occupying commanding positions on the elevated ranges to intercept escape or retreat. A strong body of the foot force, fully armed, swept down the gully in extended line, attended by a corps of light infantry traps in loose attire, like greyhounds in the slip, ready to rush from the leash as the quarry started. But the orders of the officers could not be heard from the loud and continuous roars of 'Joe! Joe! Joe!'— 'Curse the Government!—the beaks, the traps, commissioners, and all'—'the robbers,'—'the bush-rangers,' and every other vile epithet that could be remembered, almost into their ears. At length the excitement got perfectly wild as a smart fellow, closely pursued by the men-hounds, took a line of the gulley cut up with yawning holes, from which the cross planks had been purposely removed; every extraordinary spring just carrying him beyond the grasp of capture, his tracks being filled the instant he left them, and the outstretched arm of the trap within an inch of seizure in the following leap. I myself was strangely inoculated with the nervous quiver of excitement, and I think I gave an involuntary cheer as the game and mettle of the digger began to tell. But there arose a terrific menacing outcry of 'Shame! shame!—treachery!—meanness!' which a glance in the direction of the general gaze showed me was caused by a charge of the mounted men on the high ground to head back the poor fugitive. I really thought a conflict would have ensued, for there was a mad rush to the point where the collision was likely to take place, and fierce vows of vengeance registered by many a stalwart fellow who bounded past me to join in the fray. A moment after the mounted men wheeled at a sharp angle, and a fresh shout arose as another smart young fellow flew before them with almost supernatural fleetness, like a fresh hare started as the hunted one was on the point of being run down. I marvelled to see him keep the unbroken ground with the gulley at his side impracticable for cavalry; but no, he made straight on for a bunch of tents with a speed I never saw equalled by a pedestrian. It was even betting, too, that he would have reached the screen first, when lo! he stopped short so suddenly as only just to escape being ridden down by the Commissioner—the Cardigan of the charge—who seized him by the shirt collar in passing.

The rush of diggers now became diverted to the
scene of caption. I hurried forward there too,
although fearing I should witness the shedding of
blood and the sacrifice of human life ; but as I
approached I was agreeably disappointed at hearing
loud roars of laughter, and jeering outbursts of ' Joe !
Joe !' amidst which the crowd opened out a passage
for the crest-fallen heroes, who rode away under such
a salute of opprobrious epithets as I never heard
before, for the young fellow who led them off the idle
chase stopped short the moment he saw the real
fugitive was safe, coolly inquiring of his captor ' what
crime he was guilty of to be hunted like a felon.'
' Your license, you scoundrel !' was the curt reply.
Upon which he put his hand in his pocket and pulled
out the document, to the ineffable disgust of their
high mightinesses, who in grasping at the shadow had
lost the substance.

" It was a capital ruse, adopted in an emergency,
and played with greater skill than if there had been
a regular rehearsal. I flatter myself that I am a
loyal man on the average, and a respectable upholder
of law and order ; but I was unable to repress an
emotion of gratification at the result of the chase, or
an impulse of hero worship, as I sought the sole actor
in the successful diversion to offer my congratula-
tions. The myrmidons of the law now moved up
the middle of the gully in close order, attended by
anything but an admiring cortége, who made it a

point never to let the cry of ' Joe! Joe!' subside for
a moment. Occasionally a license was demanded,
and its production was the signal for fresh outbursts
of the tumult ; but the ' license meet' was brought to
a close by two other successful feints that were
played off by a pair of diggers, who simulated a
guilty timidity and dropped themselves in a slide
down their ropes into the bottoms of their wet holes,
followed by a brace of traps with dashing gallantry,
who chased them into the muddy drives, where the
lurkers purposely crawled to lead their pursuers
into the muck. Of course they were hauled up in
triumph, but the hallelujahs were quickly superseded
by choking screams of ' Joe! Joe!' when the
prisoners produced their digging warrants. The
Commissioner did not venture on another 'throw off,'
but moved away sullenly with his forces to the tune
of ' Joe! Joe! Joe!' and expressions of regret 'that
he would have to drink the Royal Family's health
after dinner at his own expense,' and such-like
observations."

Another aspect of the digger-hunting process is
given by Mr. R. M. Sergeant, correspondent of the
Geelong Advertiser :—

" ' Traps! traps! Joe! Joe!' were the well-known
signals which announced that the police were out
on a license raid. The hasty abandonment of tubs
and cradles by fossickers and outsiders, and the great
rush of shepherds to the deep holes on the flat as the

police hove in view, readily told that there were not
a few among them who believed in the doctrine that
'base is the slave who pays.'   Hunting the digger
was evidently regarded by Commissioner Sleuth and
his hounds as a source of delightful recreation, and
one of such paramount importance to the State that
the sport was reduced to an exact science.   Thus,
giving a couple of dirty constables in diggers' disguise
jumping a claim, the gentle shepherd approaches, with
dilapidated shovel on shoulder, and proceeds to dis-
possess intruders in a summary manner.   A great
barney ensues.   The constable and his mate talk big,
a crowd gathers round, and 'A ring! a ring!' is the
cry.   The combatants have just commenced to shape
when the signal referred to at the head of this para-
graph rings through the flat.   On come the traps in
skirmishing order, driving in the stragglers as they
advance, and supported by mounted troopers in the
rear, who occupy commanding positions in the
ranges.   A great haul is made, and some sixty
prisoners are marched off in triumph to the camp,
handcuffed together like a lot of felons, there to be
dealt with according to the caprice or cupidity of their
pursuers."

   Raffello, in his history of the Ballarat riot, says :—
" At the shouting of 'Joe! Joe!' the diggers without
licenses make for the deep shaft, and leave a licensed
mate or two at the windlass.   The diggers were
besieged by a regiment of troopers, and traps under

their protection would venture into the holes. The sight of the rich-looking washing stuff in possession of some lucky diggers aroused the cupidity of the police, and often made them blind to the condition of the unfortunate ones. Some of the traps were civil enough, and felt the shame of the duty, but others enjoyed the fun. The authorities generally treated the diggers very harshly. Troopers would scour the neighbouring bush, and all the unfortunate diggers they captured were tied to the stumps of trees, and left there until the hunt was over, when the captives were collected and taken to the depôt which the traps established in order to bring together the whole of their victims. From there the batch of prisoners were marched off to the camp, and fined £5, or imprisoned. So much for the unlicensed digger. The digger who wished to obtain a license was obliged to travel a few miles, and then was often kept waiting at the Commissioner's tent for two or three hours."

CHAPTER VI.

BEGINNINGS OF REVOLT.

THE arbitrary conduct on the part of the officials became at length intolerable. A change in the social organisation on the gold-fields, which was visible in 1853, enabled the diggers to agitate systematically for the repeal of the license fee. During the first two years of gold-seeking in Victoria the fields were thronged with diggers, who, like adventurous birds of passage, came expecting to pick up treasures in rich lumps, and return at once with a fortune. Many realised their hopes, and others, meeting with discouragements, abandoned the pursuit, so that gold-mining became an occupation followed by men as a settled means of earning a livelihood. Then the bitter feelings against the "exorbitant" license fee were shown in grim earnest.

An outbreak occurred on the Ovens in January 1853, in which an Assistant Commissioner was roughly handled by the diggers. In May, at Forest Creek, a disturbance arose, owing to the unjust action (so the diggers said) of a trooper, and it was not quelled until the military and police were called out to restore order. Great indignation meetings were held at Bendigo, a few months later, to call attention to the continued mismanagement of the gold-fields, and almost simultaneously the Ballarat miners commenced their demonstrations of war against the license fee.

Dissatisfaction and discontent prevailed nearly everywhere; still the Commissioners did not relax their obnoxious compulsory means of collecting the tax. The persistency of the officials' harshness, and the conduct of the Government in upholding it, were taken by many diggers as indications of their being regarded as a despicable portion of the population. But this idea was dispelled for a time, when it became known that the Governor of the colony intended to visit the gold-fields.

Sir Charles Hotham made the promised tour about the middle of 1854, and in spite of existing grievances he was most cordially received everywhere. An amusing episode of his visit is described by Mr. W. Kelly as follows :—

AN IRISH GALLANT.

" As soon as the modest cortége of the vice-regal party was discerned by the expectant diggers, there arose a loud shout of welcome, which was echoed and re-echoed from hill and glen, from flat and gully,

until all Ballarat was one wild hurrah of rejoicing.
The first impulse of the people was to detach the
horses from the carriage and draw it themselves, but
against this proceeding Sir Charles protested with
complimentary tact, to the effect that he wished to
see people more suitably employed than as beasts
of burden. The sentiment was duly appreciated and
responded to by a genuine cheer, a Milesian giant—
the leader of the multitude—at the same time
thrusting his arm into the carriage and shaking his
Excellency lustily by the hand. Sir Charles then
requested his Irish friend to direct the carriage
towards some of the best of the adjacent gullies,
and when it had proceeded as far as the horses
could find firm footing, both he and Lady Hotham
descended, while every hat, cap, and caubeen in the
crowd ascended on the wings of a roar of ecstasy.
Sir Charles took his lady on his arm, having a large
crook-headed stick in the opposite hand, but of this
his Milesian friend very quickly and unceremoniously
deprived him to keep a lane open for their advance,
addressing humorous apostrophes to the people and
their distinguished visitors, which relieved the procession of all dullness and formality ; and on coming
to a muddy space where the path was too miry to
walk over, having no cloak or coat to throw under
her footsteps, like a courtly knight of yore, he
caught up Lady Hotham bodily, with true impulsive
gallantry, and seating her on his shoulder, carried

her across amidst a tumult of admiration quite impossible to describe.

" Come to Canadian Gully, buckets of rich washing-stuff were hoisted up from the claim, and examined by Sir Charles, who was astonished at seeing numerous golden particles in the dirt. One fine nugget challenged particular observation, and this Pat picked out with his fingers, and presented in a most gracious manner to Lady Hotham, although he had no interest whatever in the claim. The operation of puddling and cradling was gone through, to the great satisfaction of the vice-regal pair, who expressed their warm thanks, Sir Charles emphatically asking, 'What can I do for you, my friends, in return for your kindness?' whereupon the ready-witted Celt, bowing respectfully, impressively replied, 'Abolish the license tax.' This was the signal for renewed cheering ; and as there was an expressed anxiety to have a reply, Sir Charles informed the multitude that if they would accompany him to the camp, where he intended to address them, they would learn his sentiments on the matter.

" Well, they did accompany him, and listened with evident satisfaction to the deliberate expressions of their Governor on that occasion. After making a tour of the gold-fields, the Governor parted with the diggers on the best possible terms."

REFORM LEAGUES.

Meanwhile the Government maintained the licensing in its fullest extent. In October 1854 the police received orders to go out twice a-week in search of unlicensed diggers. There were then four Commissioners at Ballarat, between whom the superintendence of the surrounding gold-fields was divided, but so ill-defined were the boundaries of each district that the police in their raids went over the same ground more than once, and thus unnecessarily roused the anger of the diggers by repeatedly bailing up a "mate," or by compelling the production of a license over and over again on the same day.

These stringent measures of the authorities served to bring the diggers into closer union with one another. By the organising of reform leagues and committees the whole population became educated to a certain degree in the discussion of their grievances, and several men then came to the front who in subsequent years became popular political and social leaders. Among the changes contemplated by the reform league at Ballarat may be mentioned :—
(1) Fair representation ; (2) manhood suffrage ; (3) no property qualification for Members of Legislative Council ; (4) payment of Members, and short duration of Parliaments. But its immediate object was to obtain a change in the management of the gold-

fields—the disbanding of Commissioners, and the abolition of diggers' and storekeepers' license taxes.

The motives that prompted the diggers to oppose the impost were never so unreservedly displayed as at their public meetings; the telling speeches of those "gifted with the gab" often heated the swelling emotions of the listening multitude to almost a bursting point. A lively view of a diggers' meeting is thus depicted by Mr. W. Kelly :—" At length a bell commenced ringing in front of a large tenement, and all the different groups commingled in one advancing crowd towards the entrance. I found inside an extemporised platform at the end, on to which I was ushered to a prominent place. The proposers occupied a front row, striving to look as if they were not aware of their being about to be asked to take part in the proceedings, while I could clearly see they were in communion with their memories, calling to mind the concluding words in pages so-and-so, and the starting word in the sentences on the other leaves. The seconders were in their proper position, got up without starch for the occasion, all of the 'unaccustomed as I am' class. The chairman, Mr. H—ff—y, was voted to his post by acclamation, and Dr. C——r 'broke open the ball.' He had evidently read up for the occasion, but studied harangues. Abstruse political theories and polemical refinements are not the fitting elements for popular oratory; his loftiest flights and his most

studied cadences (none of them approaching medioc-
rity, by the way) scarcely produced a fitful 'hear.'
It was evident that the audience paid no attention
to the contrasting illustrations between direct or
indirect taxation, or the grand theory of 'basing
representation on population instead of property;'
even the reference to 'unlocking the lands' elicited
only a languid meed of approbation. But when a
digger from the crowd asked aloud, 'What about
the b—y license tax?' there arose a simultaneous
shout as if from a roaring giant, which broke the
doctor's thread. He tried to stagger on, but after
a few stumbles he 'declined occupying any more of
their valuable time,' and sat down, to the apparent
delight of the whole crowd. The next speaker, and
the next, and the next, and the next still, were all of
a piece, and the cry of 'Shut up!' became impar-
tially applicable to all, until a rough, determined,
yet good-countenanced man, was lifted up in front.
He evidently did not court the prominence, but there
was no mistaking it ; he was perfectly self-possessed,
his mind was full, and his undisciplined tongue 'was
all there.' He looked steadily around with his great
hand thrust into the breast of his open shirt, where
the mud-spattered hair was evident as his whiskers.
I felt sure I knew what was coming, and his first
clearly-pronounced words, 'Brother Diggers!' made
the assurance doubly sure. He bade them be of a
good heart, but to be *united*—emphasising the word.

He advised them to obey the law, but denied the legality of the license tax, which bore down upon the industry that made the country great, and went on pampering their persecutors. He drew a most graphic picture of the tyranny of officials' enormities of digger-hunting, and wound up by swearing ' while he would die for his Queen, he would shed the last drop of his blood before he would pay another license.' The burst of enthusiasm that followed this declaration is altogether indescribable. It seemed to lift the great tent into mid-air ; and, inoculated with the glow of feeling around me, I could almost imagine that I had a cloud for a footstool. The speaker was seized, *nolo episcopari* notwithstanding, and carried out in triumph to the open air, leaving the chairman to dissolve the meeting, vote himself thanks, and all the rest of it. It was then, in truth, the *bonâ-fide* meeting commenced, and many a spirit-stirring speech bearing close upon the one text was delivered extemporaneously from the head of a barrel or the end of a waggon."

The ill-will manifested at these gatherings was kept fervid by the official tyranny which yet accompanied the collecting of the tax, and its virulence was much increased when the diggers learned that the authorities employed informers whose histories precluded the possibility of their acting truthfully, and stamped them as men of straw, ready to swear to anything at the official's bidding. Such a state of affairs so irritated the men as to cause the more excitable to collect arms. Men of different nationalities formed separate leagues ; while throughout the whole digging community the probability of open insurrection was commonly discussed.

CHAPTER VII.

A T last an incident caused the long-smouldering elements of disaffection to burst out suddenly in a blaze of infuriated indignation.

A digger named Scobie met an old chum of his, and being overjoyed at the unexpected re-union, hastened to show his good-fellowship by "shouting." In the course of the day the two became drunk, and attempted to enter Bentley's Eureka Hotel. Being refused admittance, Scobie got troublesome. An altercation ensued with the people of the hotel, during which his head was split open with a spade. The blow killed him. Bentley's Hotel was held in disrepute by respectable miners, and its proprietor was considered a bad character. An inquest was held on the body of the murdered man. It was not conducted with the care and discrimination which should attend such an inquiry. The coroner's verdict, "that the deceased died from the effects of a wound inflicted by a person unknown," was so at variance with public opinion, that another official investigation was held, which indicted Bentley for the killing of Scobie. At the police court the land-lord was acquitted, but the manner in which the case was conducted made it patent to all that justice had been trifled with. The Police Magistrate was known to be intimate with the prisoner, and was believed to be a sharer in his illicit gains. The trial was so injudicially carried out, that the Junior Commissioner, Mr. Johnston, took copies of the evidence and forwarded them to the Attorney-General.

The diggers became furious upon hearing of this acquittal, and on the 17th October 1854 assembled in great numbers around Bentley's Hotel. They expressed dissatisfaction at the result of the trial, and subscribed money for the purposes of bringing the case before more competent authorities, and of offering a reward for the capture of the dastardly murderers of Scobie. Soldiers were told off to the gathering to nip in the bud any rebellious exhibitions of wrath. While the diggers moved round the spot, listening to indignant invectives of their spokesmen, a lad in the crowd threw a stone which narrowly missed a trooper, and smashed into pieces a pane of the lamp in front of the hotel. The police immediately tried to arrest the offender, and then the surging crowd gave free vent to its feelings. Stones and missiles of all kinds were thrown until every window in the hotel was broken into atoms. Madly infuriated, they rushed against the front door, almost battering it to pieces; and whilst the tumultuous crowd were attacking the front of the building, a man with a bundle of paper and other inflammable materials got into the bowling-alley at the rear and set the place on fire. The soldiers made strenuous efforts to disperse the people and save the hotel; but all in vain. Bentley succeeded in escaping during the melée, and on a swift horse rode to the Commissioners' camp for additional assistance. Presently more soldiers arrived on the scene, but it was too late to stop the flames, which had by this time taken a firm hold of the building. The immense blaze drew from the gravel pits all the diggers, excepting those who happened to be below and were unable to come up to the surface without the help of their mates at the windlass, who had impetuously left their posts in order to take part in the demonstration against officialism and injustice. The enveloping flames continued the work of destruction by greedily licking up the wooden beams and heavy columns, and finished by reducing the whole building to a spread of ashes.

For setting fire to the hotel three men well known on the diggings were arrested. This so incensed the diggers that they meditated an attack on the Commissioners' camp and a forcible release of the prisoners. However, after a time milder propositions prevailed, and it was agreed that nine

of the diggers should offer bail. Accordingly, a
deputation from the diggers went to the Commissioners, and succeeded in bringing away the
three men, although at first the turbulence of the
crowd led the officials to think that the offer of
bail was merely a *ruse* to rescue the prisoners by
force while the bail-bonds were being prepared.
When the deputation came out of the camp with
the three released captives, the crowd of diggers
greeted them with such an impetuous rush that it
required the prompt efforts of both the deputation
and its charge to prevent a collision with the
soldiers. A monster indignation meeting followed,
at which the diggers collected £200 to be paid to
the discoverer of the murderer of Scobie. They
would have collected more had not the Government
also offered a reward and as well rearrested Bentley,
who this time was tried, convicted, and sentenced
to three years' hard labour. The corrupt Police
Magistrate shortly afterwards departed for more
congenial scenes.

The trial of the three men for the burning of the
hotel was held in Melbourne, and a number of the
diggers attended. The prisoners were convicted, but
with a strong recommendation to mercy, the jury
adding that they would not have had their painful
duty to perform if those entrusted with the government at Ballarat had done their duty properly.
This rider to the verdict was received with loud

and prolonged cheering by the crowded court. The three men were severally sentenced to three, four, and six months' imprisonment. This sentence was considered so unjust by the diggers that they promptly sent delegates to Melbourne to demand the release of the prisoners.

On the 27th of November the deputation (Messrs. Humffray, Kennedy, and Black) waited upon His Excellency the Governor. He listened to their remonstrances, but was so displeased with the haughty tone assumed by them that he said, as representative of Her Majesty, he could not allow their peremptory demand. However, it was intimated that if a proper memorial was sent to the Government the prisoners might be released from custody. But the delegates were forbidden by the indignant diggers to plead with the authorities, and therefore returned, leaving the object of their mission unattained. The people on the diggings were further incensed at this failure, and many now busied themselves in preparing arms and ammunition, while committees and leagues sat night and day.

The Government expected a violent outbreak of passion, and made preparations for eventualities by concentrating all available troops at Ballarat. The ill-feeling of the gold-fields' population soon manifested itself, several detachments of troops being pelted with mud and other missiles while marching along the diggings' thoroughfares. On the 28th of

November, as a party of soldiers from Melbourne were approaching the camp at Ballarat, some diggers in ambush suddenly made a raid on the military waggons, in the hope of obtaining arms. They wounded a few soldiers, and managed to overturn several waggons and rifle their contents. But when in the vicinity of their camp the soldiers rallied, and, with the assistance of the mounted police, put the marauders to flight, wounding some of them. A crowd of men from the surrounding gullies left their tents and came up to see the conflict, but were soon driven away panic-stricken. It was eleven o'clock before the troops quartered, but the noise made by the diggers in keeping up huge fires, and continually discharging fire-arms, prevented them from obtaining any rest that night.

A LOYAL TOAST.

An episode which occurred on that turbulent evening shows the general feeling of dissatisfaction at the conduct of the officials. It is related by Mr. Samuel Irwin, a correspondent of the *Geelong Advertiser* :—

"A dinner was given by the American residents of Ballarat to the American Consul, and most of the leading residents of all nationalities were there. Just as the toasts were about to be proposed, a message was received by Mr. Commissioner Rede, stating that an attack had been made on some troops coming from Melbourne when they reached the workings on the Eureka lead. The Commissioner and other officials withdrew at once, as the report was that several lives had been lost. When the toast of the Queen was proposed, a significant fact was disclosed—for several minutes no one would respond to it. The duty of responding had originally been allotted to the resident Commissioner, who had left for the scene of the outrage. Many British subjects (business men and miners) were present, yet they sat without the slightest attempt to show their loyalty until the chairman said if no British subject would volunteer for the duty, he must do so himself. At length a gentleman undertook to respond. He very pithily said, 'While I and my fellow-colonists claim to be and are thoroughly loyal to our Sovereign Lady the Queen, we do not and will not respect her man-servants, her maid-servants, her oxen, or her *asses.*' The last word was delivered with an emphasis, and received with tumultuous applause."

BURNING THE LICENSES.

We learn from Withers' *History of Ballarat* that a monstre meeting was called by the reform league for the 29th of November, on Bakery Hill, at which some thousands were expected from Creswick,

besides delegates from all the other gold-fields;
for the movement had now become general, and
emissaries had been sent all over the colony to
enlist sympathy, procure help, and, in fact, make
the rising national, if not revolutionary. At the
meeting on the 29th, Humffray and the other
delegates (Black and Kennedy) gave in their report
of the conference with the Governor.

Some 12,000 men, it is said, were present at the
meeting. A platform was erected, and on a flagstaff
was hung the insurgent flag—the Southern Cross.
The flag had a blue ground, on which, in silver,
the four principal stars of the constellation of the
Southern Cross were shown. Mr. Hayes was the
chairman, and the site of the meeting was on the
adjoining area, now occupied by Victoria Street,
between East and Humffray Streets. Besides the
committee of the league and the delegates, there
were reporters on the platform, and two Roman
Catholic priests—the Rev. Fathers Downing and
Smyth. The Catholic Bishop had also come to help
to maintain peace.

Resolutions condemnatory of the action of the
authorities were adopted unanimously. It was
proposed :—"That this meeting, being convinced
that the obnoxious license fee is an imposition, and
an unjustifiable tax on free labour, pledges itself to
take immediate steps to abolish the same by at once
burning all their licenses. That, in the event of any

party being arrested for having no licenses, the united people will, under all circumstances, defend and protect them."

And again :—"That as the diggers have to pay no licenses, it is necessary for them to be prepared for the contingency, as it would be utterly inconsistent, after refusing to pay a license, to call in a Commissioner for the adjustment of such disputes ; and this meeting resolves, whenever any party or parties have a dispute, the parties so disputing shall each appoint one man, the two men thus appointed to call in a third, and these three to decide the case finally."

Mr. Humffray proposed, and Mr. Kennedy seconded :—" That this meeting protests against the common practice of bodies of military marching into a peaceable district with fixed bayonets, and also any force, police or otherwise, firing on the people, under any circumstances, without the previous reading of the Riot Act ; and that if Government officials continue to act thus unconstitutionally, we cannot be responsible for similar or worse deeds from the people."

The proposals were received with acclamation, and carried vociferously ; and had it not been for the chairman and his supporters' interference, the men that ventured to hint of milder and more constitutional measures would have been torn limb from limb by the infuriated diggers.

Bonfires were made of licenses; guns and revolvers were discharged; and league tickets of membership were issued to the crowd. Troops were under arms in the gully beneath the camp all the time, waiting in readiness for an outbreak.

THE LAST DIGGER-HUNT.

"With incredible want of prudence, the authorities chose the juncture marked by the meeting of the 29th of November for a more irritating display than usual of the so long condemned practice of digger-hunting. On the 30th of November the last raid of this kind in Victoria occurred, under the direction of Commissioners Rede and Johnston, and the authorities by that act destroyed the remaining influence of the friends of moral force among the diggers. The police, supported by the whole military force available, with skirmishers in advance and cavalry on the flanks, formed on the flat south of the camp, and advanced upon the Gravel Pits, as the Bakery Hill diggings were called. This cleared the swarming crowd of diggers collected there, the diggers retiring as the troops advanced At certain parts of the main road, however, the diggers made a stand, and received the troops with a running fire of stones and occasional gun-shots. The troops took some prisoners, and returned to the camp. Soon after that the Southern Cross was again hoisted on

Bakery Hill ; the diggers knelt round the flag, swore mutual defence, and implored the help of God. New leaders came to the front, as the advocates of moral force were discomfited by the authorities and the more turbulent insurgents." Peter Lalor, a native of the Queen's County, Ireland, who has since become one of our most prominent and respected legislators, assumed a foremost position at this dangerous turn of affairs. A fiery-spirited Italian, named Carboni Raffello, was another who then placed himself in the front rank of the diggers' movement.

CHAPTER VIII.

THE EUREKA STOCKADE.

THE insurgents had pitched upon the junction of the Eureka lead with the Melbourne road as a place suitable for meeting *en masse*. About an acre of the ground was roughly enclosed with slabs, and within this area the diggers commenced their drilling. The slabs were put up as a screen merely, so that the preparations for revolt might not be too closely watched. This frail enclosure received the name of the Eureka Stockade.

Lalor delivered a speech within this stockade. It was couched thus:—" Gentlemen, I find myself in this responsible position for the following reasons. Outraged at the unaccountable conduct of the camp officials in the wicked license-hunt at the point of the bayonet, the diggers took it as an insult to their manhood, and a challenge to the determination expressed at their monstre meeting. They ran to arms, and crowded on Bakery Hill. They wanted a leader, but no one came forward, and confusion was the consequence. I mounted the stump, and called on the people to fall in into divisions according to the arms they had got, and to choose their captains out of the best men among themselves. My call was answered with unanimous acclamation, and complied to with willing obedience. The result is, I have been able to bring about that order without which it would be folly to face the impending struggle like men. I make no pretentions to military knowledge. I have not the presumption to assume the chief command no more than any other man who means well in the cause of the diggers. I shall be glad to see the best man take the lead. In fact, gentlemen, I expected someone who is really well known to you to come forward and direct our movement! However, if you appoint me your commander-in-chief, I shall not shrink; I mean to do my duty as a man. I tell you that if once I pledge my hand to the diggers, I will neither defile it by treachery nor render it contemptible by cowardice."

Raffello, who had a great admiration for Lalor's straightforwardness and many other manly qualities, comments thus :—" Bravo, Peter, you gave us your hand on the Eureka, and left there your arm," an incontestible proof of the sincerity of Lalor's pledge.

Lalor was appointed commander-in-chief. In thanking the council for the confidence placed in him, he told them he was determined to prepare the diggers to resist force by force ; but at the same time it was perfectly understood by every-

11

one present that the organisation was solely for defence.

In the stockade a straight pole, eighty feet long, was erected to serve as a flag-staff. At the head of this the diggers hoisted their standard—the Southern Cross. Then Lalor, gun in hand, mounted a stump. Resting the stock of the gun on his foot, and grasping its barrel firmly in his left hand, he slowly raised his right arm towards the standard, and proceeded solemnly to swear in the diggers. He said, " It is my duty to take from you the oath to be faithful to the standard. The man who, after this solemn oath, does not stand by our standard is a coward at heart." All those who did not intend to take part in the insurrection were ordered to leave the meeting. Then the armed diggers, numbering about five hundred, gathered around the flag-staff. They were formed into divisions, and the captains of each saluted their commander-in-chief. He now knelt down, and solemnly pointing to the standard streaming in the breeze, said, in firm, serious, and glowing tones, " We swear by the standard to stand truly by each other and fight to defend our rights and liberties ;" to which the diggers responded decisively by a universal " Amen," and by simultaneously stretching five hundred hands towards the flag.

Immediately after the swearing-in ceremony the names were taken down and the men formed into squads for drill. Drilling was kept up with but little intermission till a late hour, and was now and then renewed up to the capture of the stockade. Side by side with these warlike preparations several claims were being worked ; indeed, some of the working miners gave up their tents as quarters for insurgent officers.

Orders of war were sent round the diggings to obtain arms, ammunition, etc. Lalor was obliged to keep piquets to enforce these orders, and also to prevent their being made a cover for robbery, because some unscrupulous diggers had, in the name of the insurgents, pillaged the storekeepers. The levying officers issued receipts on behalf of the Reform League. Some of these are rather entertaining documents. Here is one : "Received from the Ballarat store, 1 Pistol for the Comtee x. Hugh McCarty—Hurrah for the people!" Another : "The Reform Lege Comete, 4 drenks, fower chillings, 4 Pics, for fower of thee neight watch troops xP." The four night watch troops were some of those insurgents told off to patrol the diggings. The foragers, as things came to a crisis, became more peremptory in their demands, one party even threatening to shoot a storekeeper if he did not hand over quickly. But, notwithstanding the levying, the insurgents failed to obtain sufficient war material. Several of their fire-arms were afterwards found loaded with pebbles and such missiles.

Lalor's men kept together within the stockade, some cooking the meat which friendly butchers had brought in ; others mending muskets or making pikes or similar rude weapons for use by the several companies of pikemen. Friends and enemies also dropped into the stockade at all hours until the day before the tragic event.

Humffray, ever foremost in advocating peaceful reform, heard, when in the stockade, of a project to attack the soldiers' camp. It was thought that 2000 diggers could be got for that purpose. Humffray, with other mild spirits, vainly endeavoured to persuade them from attempting it, and then left the stockade.

Vinegar Hill was the pass-word on the night of the 2nd of December, and its ominous associations led several to abandon what they saw was a badly-organised and hopeless movement.

Meanwhile the soldiers had not been idle. After securing a commanding position on the rising ground afterwards known as "Soldiers' Hill," they vigilantly watched the movements of the insurgents. The police were also on the alert, so that little was said or done among the insurgents that was not soon afterwards reported to the authorities.

A Government officer, then in the camp, writes :—

"On the 1st of December the Government took final measures to meet the assault. Every Government employee was armed and told off to his post, and sentinels and videttes were placed at every point. The principal buildings of the camp were fortified with breastworks of firewood, trusses of hay, and bags of corn from the Commissariat Stores, and the women and children were sent for security into the store, which was walled with thick slabs and accounted bullet-proof. A violent storm of rain, with thunder, commenced as these arrangements were completed, and the mounted police, soaked through with rain, spent the night standing or lying by their horses, armed, and horses saddled ready for instant action. At four A.M. on the 2nd of December the whole garrison was under arms, and soon after daylight a demonstration in force was made towards Bakery Hill without opposition, although bodies of men were seen drilling near the Red Hill. A mounted trooper coming from Melbourne with despatches was fired at near the Eureka lead. No work was carried on through the entire diggings, and every place of business was closed. Notices were issued stating that if any lights were seen in the neighbourhood after eight o'clock at night, or if any fire-arms were discharged, the offenders would be fired at by the military." The same Government officer writes about the

STORMING OF THE STOCKADE.

"Before daylight on the morning of the 3rd of December a mixed force of two hundred and seventy-six men, including a strong body of cavalry, quietly left the camp for the purpose of taking the stockade. At early dawn they reached the neighbourhood of the position sought, and the advance files were fired at by a sentinel within the stockade. The order to attack was given, and the 40th regiment, led by Captain Thomas, the chief officer in command, made a quick advance upon the double breastwork which formed the stronghold of the insurgents. After several volleys had been fired on both sides, a barrier of ropes, slabs, and overturned carts was crossed, and the defenders driven out or into the shallow pits with which the place was spotted, and in which many were put to death in the first heat of the conflict either by bullets or by bayonet thrusts."

Raffello says—"I awoke on Sunday morning. A discharge of musketry—then a round from a bugle—the command 'Forward'—and another discharge of musketry was sharply kept up by the red-coats for a couple of minutes. The shots whizzed by my tent. I jumped out of my stretcher and rushed to my chimney facing the stockade. The force within could not muster then above one hundred and fifty diggers. The shepherds' holes inside the lower part of the stockade were turned into rifle pits. . . The dragoons from the south and troopers from the north were trotting at full speed towards the stockade. Peter Lalor was on top of the first logged-up hole within the stockade, and by his decided gestures pointed to the men to retire among the holes. He was shot down in his shoulder at this identical moment. It was a chance shot. I recollect it well, for the discharge of musketry from the military now mowed down all who had heads above the barricades. ... Those who suffered most were the pikemen, who stood their ground from the time the whole division had been posted on top, facing the Melbourne road from Ballarat, in double file under the slabs to stick the cavalry with their pikes. The old command 'Charge' was distinctly heard, and the red-coats ran with fixed bayonets to storm the stockade. A few cuts and kicks, a little pulling down, and the job was done; too quickly for their wonted ardour, for they actually thrust their bayonets through the bodies of the dead and wounded strewed about the ground. A wild hurrah burst out, and the 'Southern Cross' was torn down. Of the armed diggers, some made off the best way they could, others surrendered themselves as prisoners, and were collected in groups and marched down the gully. . . . The red-coats were now ordered to 'fall in,' their bloody work being over, and were marched off, dragging with them the 'Southern Cross.'"

In less than twenty-five minutes the engagement was over, and the soldiers had possession of the stockade and one hundred and twenty-five prisoners. During the same day the soldiers who were killed in the inglorious conflict were buried in the cemetery;

and no opposition was offered to the dead bodies of the insurgents being placed in rough coffins and taken away by their sorrowing friends.

After the fray notices were posted up at various places ordering all well-disposed persons to return to their ordinary occupations, and to abstain from assembling in large groups. The soldiers then returned to their camp, but remained under arms all night, rumours of an intended attack keeping them on the alert, although it was tiring work; and most of them, having had no repose for four nights, were almost exhausted.

On the next evening a number of insurgents, favoured by a clouded moon, crept up under the cover of the nearest tent beyond the palisade and fired from several points upon the sentinels. This caused a sudden alarm in the camp; everyone ran to his post, and a general firing followed, resulting in the wounding of a woman and child in one of the tents and of three men on the road close by, who unfortunately happened to be passing.

On the 5th of December Major-General Sir Robert Nickle arrived with a relief contingent from Melbourne, and later in the day a force of eight hundred soldiers and a large party of seamen from the men-of-war then in the bay still further strengthened the hands of the Government. The presence of these additional troops had immediate effect throughout the digging community in sinking below zero the spirit of insurrection, which was already depressed by the loss of the Eureka stockade. Sir Robert was a veteran well skilled in quelling disturbances. The district was now under martial law, but his good sense made it more acceptable to the diggers than the previous administration of the Commissioners.

The soldiers were kept at Ballarat until affairs on the gold-fields resumed a more peaceful course; then, as no further tumults were apprehended, Sir Robert Nickle and his forces returned to Melbourne, leaving a small garrison to await the turn of events.

EXCITEMENT IN MELBOURNE.

Meanwhile, the Government were making other strenuous efforts to restore order, and favouring the report that the leaders of the revolutionary movement were foreigners, issued notices, calling upon British subjects not only to abstain from identifying themselves with persons who were endeavouring to excite the mining population to riotous courses, but to render support and assistance to the authorities, civil and military, then stationed at Ballarat. At the same time £500 was offered for the arrest of a German named Vern, whom the Government believed to be the chief instigator of the outbreak. Civilians in Melbourne, Geelong, and various towns in the colony were requested to come forward and be sworn in as special constables.

From McCombie's *History of Victoria* we learn:—
"That the Legislative Council presented to the
Governor an address expressing their sympathy for
him and pledging their support to him while affairs
were so embarrassing." Sir Charles Hotham replied,
"That the firm resolve to suppress the incipient
revolution was softened by the readiness with which
he offered to redress the grievances complained of.
It would be his constant endeavour to conduct the
Government with the utmost possible temper. The
time for military rule had passed, but when there was
an outbreak, and that caused by foreigners—men
who had not been suffered to remain in their own
country in consequence of the violence of their
character—then Englishmen must sink all minor
differences and unite to support the authorities."

The Government, however, fared differently when
a direct appeal was made to the people. At
Melbourne a public meeting had been called by
requisition to consider the best means for protecting
the city during the crisis at the diggings. The
principal agitators in this matter seemed to be the
members of the Legislature, who took a large share
in the proceedings of this public meeting. The
resolutions proposed were received with such ill-
concealed dissatisfaction that, after the Mayor had
declared two of them to be carried, the opponents
of the Government interfered, and such confusion
prevailed that the gentleman who presided vacated

the chair; and a series of resolutions, diametrically opposed to the proceedings of the Executive, and demanding an immediate settlement of the differences between the Government and the diggers, were carried with the utmost enthusiasm. One speaker told the people they must go forth with their brother-diggers to conquer or die.

" The Government demonstration having terminated in so unsatisfactory a manner, another meeting was convened on the following day, ' for the assertion of order and the protection of constitutional liberty.' It took place on a large open space of ground near St. Paul's Church, at the corner of Flinder's Lane. From four to seven thousand people were present, the chair being filled by Henry Langlands, one of the largest employers of labour in Melbourne. The resolutions condemned the whole policy of the Government, and declared that, while disapproving of the physical resistance offered by the diggers, the meeting could not, without betraying the interests of liberty, lend its aid to the Executive until the coercive measures they were attempting to introduce should be abandoned. The result of this meeting had very considerable weight with the Executive, and the same afternoon a *Government Gazette* extraordinary appeared, in which was a proclamation revoking martial law at Ballarat."

A few days before the outbreak a Commission had been appointed to inquire into the state of the mining districts, and now, in deference to the feelings shown at the public meetings, several gentlemen were added to it, in order to find out the grounds of the diggers' complaints. The Commissioner urged the Government to grant a general amnesty as to the past; but the Government considered that some of the prisoners taken in the stockade should be tried for high treason.

A monstre meeting was therefore held in Melbourne, at which it was resolved, " That the unhappy outbreak at Ballarat was induced by no traitorous designs against the institution of monarchy, but purely by a sense of political wrong and irritation, engendered by the injudicious and offensive enforcement of an obnoxious and invidious tax, which, if legal, has since been condemned by the Commission." Thousands in Ballarat subscribed a similar petition.

But the Executive remained obdurate, and on the 18th of January issued a public notice offering £400, £200 each, for the arrest of Lalor and Black, because of their treasonable and seditions language in inciting men to take up arms against the Queen.

The insurgent chief, Lalor, was severely wounded whilst defending the stockade. He fell to the ground. Some of his pikemen seeing his body, covered it with slabs. When the soldiers retired with their prisoners, he managed to extricate himself from the *débris* and make his way to his friends. On the following day his left arm had to be amputated. He secreted himself in various friendly huts at different places, and after several narrow escapes, succeeded in eluding the police in their search for fugitives. His friends proving true to him, notwithstanding the reward of £200, he ultimately reached Geelong, where he remained until the storm of general disapproval had extinguished the desire of the authorities for his capture.

In the opinion of many, the agitation at Ballarat was constitutional at first, and had assumed its unconstitutional form in consequence of the coercion of the Commissioners, who precipitated measures by their imprudent digger-hunting during the period of excitement.

However, the Government continued the prosecution of the rioters, despite their being the objects of public sympathy. The trial was ended on the 1st of April by the jury acquitting the prisoners, a result which had been generally anticipated.

WRONGS RIGHTED.

The insurrectionists were afterwards conciliated by the efforts of the Commission of Inquiry, and consequent redress of grievances. The revolt, in addition to the valuable lives lost, cost the colony £20,000 for military expenses, extra police charges, and compensation to sufferers.

From Westgarth's *Colony of Victoria* we extract :— " The Commission produced a lengthened report, in which the whole system of gold-fields' management was proposed to be reconstituted. The miners' earnings were found to be, on an average, rather smaller than those of other branches of colonial labour—a circumstance not favourable to the persistent maintenance of a heavy license fee of practically very unequal incidence. The report recommended the abolition of this fee, and in its place the imposition of a moderate export duty on gold. The issue of a 'Miner's Right' was suggested, at a cost to each miner of one pound a-year, and conferring upon him both the mining privileges and the franchise. The title of 'Commissioner' to the head of each gold-field, a name now associated with the wranglings of the past, was proposed to be changed to the old English mining title, 'Warden.' The Commissioners recommended local elective mining courts, and benches of local unpaid justices of the peace, who should sit with the regular paid magistrate. The more intelligent of the miners were constituted local justices of the peace, and arrangements were made by which the mining districts elected their own representatives to the 'Colonial Legislature.'"

Mr. Peter Lalor* was one of the first of these

* Recently the sum of £4000 has been voted to Mr. Lalor, on his retiring to a well-earned rest from the arduous duties attending the Speakership of a House where so many members require a strong hand and determined will to teach them the responsibilities of their position.

representatives, and has since been in several ministries, and twice Speaker of the Assembly.

Thus ended one of the few unfortunate incidents of Australian history. The miners have since been as loyal as any other section of the population, and, by their industrious delving in the seemingly inexhaustible gold mines of Victoria, they have contributed a full share towards the prosperity of the colony.

Printed by WALTER SCOTT, *Felling, Newcastle-on-Tyne.*

Monthly Shilling Volumes.   Cloth, cut or uncut edges.

THE CAMELOT SERIES.

EDITED BY ERNEST RHYS.

VOLUMES ALREADY ISSUED—

ROMANCE OF KING ARTHUR. Edited by E. Rhys.
THOREAU'S WALDEN. Edited by W. H. Dircks.
ENGLISH OPIUM-EATER. Edited by William Sharp.
LANDOR'S CONVERSATIONS. Edited by H. Ellis.
PLUTARCH'S LIVES. Edited by B. J. Snell, M.A.
RELIGIO MEDICI, etc. Edited by J. A. Symonds.
SHELLEY'S LETTERS. Edited by Ernest Rhys.
PROSE WRITINGS OF SWIFT. Edited by W. Lewin.
MY STUDY WINDOWS. Edited by R. Garnett, LL.D.
GREAT ENGLISH PAINTERS. Edited by W. Sharp.
LORD BYRON'S LETTERS. Edited by M. Blind.
ESSAYS BY LEIGH HUNT. Edited by A. Symons.
LONGFELLOW'S PROSE. Edited by W. Tirebuck.
GREAT MUSICAL COMPOSERS. Edited by E. Sharp.
MARCUS AURELIUS. Edited by Alice Zimmern.
SPECIMEN DAYS IN AMERICA. By Walt Whitman.
WHITE'S NATURAL HISTORY of SELBORNE. Edited, with Introduction, by Richard Jefferies.
DEFOE'S SINGLETON. Edited by H. Halliday Sparling.
MAZZINI'S ESSAYS. Edited by William Clarke.
THE PROSE WRITINGS OF HEINRICH HEINE. Edited, with Introduction, by Havelock Ellis.
REYNOLDS' DISCOURSES. Edited by Helen Zimmern.
PAPERS OF STEELE & ADDISON. Edited by W. Lewin.
BURNS'S LETTERS. Edited by J. Logie Robertson, M.A.
VOLSUNGA SAGA. Edited by H. H. Sparling.
SARTOR RESARTUS Edited by Ernest Rhys.
WRITINGS OF EMERSON. Edited by Percival Chubb.
SENECA'S MORALS. Edited by Walter Clode.
DEMOCRATIC VISTAS. By Walt Whitman.
LIFE OF LORD HERBERT. Edited by Will H. Dircks.
ENGLISH PROSE Edited by Arthur Galton.
THE PILLARS OF SOCIETY, and other Plays. By Henrik Ibsen. Edited by Havelock Ellis.
FAIRY AND FOLK TALES. Edited by W. B. Yeats.
EPICTETUS. Edited by T. W. Rolleston.
THE ENGLISH POETS. By James Russell Lowell.
ESSAYS OF DR. JOHNSON. Edited by Stuart J. Reid.
ESSAYS OF WILLIAM HAZLITT. Edited by F. Carr.
LANDOR'S PENTAMERON, &c. Edited by H. Ellis.

London : WALTER SCOTT, 24 Warwick Lane, Paternoster Row.

GREAT WRITERS.

A NEW SERIES OF CRITICAL BIOGRAPHIES.

Edited by Professor Eric S. Robertson, M.A.

MONTHLY SHILLING VOLUMES.

GREAT WRITERS—(*Continued*).

LIFE OF SCOTT. By Professor Yonge.
"For readers and lovers of the poems and novels of Sir Walter Scott, this is a most enjoyable book."—*Aberdeen Free Press.*

LIFE OF BURNS. By Professor Blackie.
"The editor certainly made a hit when he persuaded Blackie to write about Burns."—*Pall Mall Gazette.*

LIFE OF VICTOR HUGO. By Frank T. Marzials.
"Mr. Marzials's volume presents to us, in a more handy form than any English, or even French handbook gives, the summary of what, up to the moment in which we write, is known or conjectured about the life of the great poet."—*Saturday Review.*

LIFE OF EMERSON. By Richard Garnett, LL.D.
"As to the larger section of the public, to whom the series of Great Writers is addressed, no record of Emerson's life and work could be more desirable, both in breadth of treatment and lucidity of style, than Dr. Garnett's."—*Saturday Review.*

LIFE OF GOETHE. By James Sime.
"Mr. James Sime's competence as a biographer of Goethe, both in respect of knowledge of his special subject, and of German literature generally, is beyond question."—*Manchester Guardian.*

LIFE OF CONGREVE. By Edmund Gosse.
"Mr. Gosse has written an admirable and most interesting biography of a man of letters who is of particular interest to other men of letters."—*The Academy.*

LIFE OF BUNYAN. By Canon Venables.
"A most intelligent, appreciative, and valuable memoir."—*Scotsman.*

LIFE OF CRABBE. By T. E. Kebbel.
"No English poet since Shakespeare has observed certain aspects of nature and of human life more closely; and in the qualities of manliness and of sincerity he is surpassed by none. . . . Mr. Kebbel's monograph is worthy of the subject."—*Athenæum.*

LIFE OF HEINE. By William Sharp.
"This is an admirable monograph. . . . more fully written up to the level of recent knowledge and criticism of its theme than any other English work."—*Scotsman.*

LIFE OF MILL. By W. L. Courtney.
"A most sympathetic and discriminating memoir."—*Glasgow Herald.*

LIFE OF SCHILLER. By Henry W. Nevison.
"This a well-written little volume, which presents the leading facts of the poet's life in a neatly rounded picture, and gives an adequate critical estimate of each of Schiller's separate works and the effect of the whole upon literature."—*Scotsman.*

Complete Bibliography to each volume, by J. P. ANDERSON, British Museum.

Volumes are in preparation by Goldwin Smith, Frederick Wedmore, Oscar Browning, Arthur Symons, W. E. Henley, Barclay Squire, Hermann Merivale, H. E. Watts, T. W. Rolleston, Cosmo Monkhouse, Dr. Garnett, Frank T. Marzials, W. H Pollock, John Addington Symonds, etc., etc.

LIBRARY EDITION OF "GREAT WRITERS."—Printed on large paper of extra quality, in handsome binding, Demy 8vo, price 2s. 6d.

London: WALTER SCOTT, 24 Warwick Lane, Paternoster Row.

The Canterbury Poets.

Edited by William Sharp.

WITH INTRODUCTORY NOTICES BY VARIOUS CONTRIBUTORS.

In SHILLING Monthly Volumes, Square 8vo. Well printed on fine toned paper, with Red-line Border, and strongly bound in Cloth. Each Volume contains from 300 to 350 pages.

Cloth, Red Edges	-	1s.	*Red Roan, Gilt Edges* 2s. 6d.	
Cloth, Uncut Edges	-	1s.	*Pad. Morocco, Gilt Edges* - 5s.	

THE FOLLOWING VOLUMES ARE NOW READY.

CHRISTIAN YEAR.
By Rev. John Keble.
COLERIDGE. Ed. by J. Skipsey.
LONGFELLOW. Ed. by E. Hope.
CAMPBELL. Edited by J. Hogben.
SHELLEY. Edited by J. Skipsey.
WORDSWORTH.
Edited by A. J. Symington.
BLAKE. Edited by Joseph Skipsey.
WHITTIER. Edited by Eva Hope.
POE. Edited by Joseph Skipsey.
CHATTERTON.
Edited by John Richmond.
BURNS. Poems. } Edited by
BURNS. Songs. } Joseph Skipsey.
MARLOWE.
Edited by P. E. Pinkerton.
KEATS. Edited by John Hogben.
HERBERT. Edited by E. Rhys.
VICTOR HUGO.
Translated by Dean Carrington.
COWPER. Edited by Eva Hope.
SHAKESPEARE.
Songs, Poems, and Sonnets.
Edited by William Sharp.
EMERSON. Edited by W. Lewin.
SONNETS of this CENTURY.
Edited by William Sharp.
WHITMAN. Edited by E. Rhys.
SCOTT. Marmion, etc.
SCOTT. Lady of the Lake, etc.
Edited by William Sharp.
PRAED. Edited by Fred. Cooper.
HOGG By his Daughter, Mrs Garden.
GOLDSMITH. Ed. by W. Tirebuck.
MACKAY'S LOVE LETTERS.
SPENSER. Edited by Hon R. Noel.
CHILDREN OF THE POETS.
Edited by Eric S. Robertson.
JONSON. Edited by J. A. Symonds.
BYRON (2 Vols.)
Edited by Mathilde Blind.
THE SONNETS OF EUROPE.
Edited by S. Waddington.

RAMSAY. Ed. by J. L. Robertson.
DOBELL. Edited by Mrs. Dobell.
DAYS OF THE YEAR.
With Introduction by Wm. Sharp.
POPE. Edited by John Hogben.
HEINE. Edited by Mrs. Kroeker.
BEAUMONT & FLETCHER.
Edited by J. S. Fletcher.
BOWLES, LAMB, &c.
Edited by William Tirebuck.
EARLY ENGLISH POETRY.
Edited by H. Macaulay Fitzgibbon.
SEA MUSIC. Edited by Mrs Sharp.
HERRICK. Edited by Ernest Rhys.
BALLADES AND RONDEAUS
Edited by J. Gleeson White.
IRISH MINSTRELSY.
Edited by H. Halliday Sparling.
MILTON'S PARADISE LOST.
Edited by J. Bradshaw, M.A., LL.D.
JACOBITE BALLADS.
Edited by G. S. Macquoid.
AUSTRALIAN BALLADS.
Edited by D. B. W. Sladen, B.A.
MOORE. Edited by John Dorrian.
BORDER BALLADS.
Edited by Graham R. Tomson.
SONG-TIDE By P. B. Marston.
ODES OF HORACE
Translations by Sir S. de Vere, Bt.
OSSIAN. Edited by G. E. Todd.
ELFIN MUSIC. Ed. by A. Waite.
SOUTHEY. Ed. by S. R. Thompson.
CHAUCER. Edited by F. N. Paton.
POEMS OF WILD LIFE.
Edited by Chas. G. D. Roberts, M.A.
PARADISE REGAINED.
Edited by J. Bradshaw, M.A., LL.D.
CRABBE. Edited by E. Lamplough.
DORA GREENWELL.
Edited by William Dorling.
GOETHE'S FAUST.
Edited by E. Craigmyle.

London : WALTER SCOTT, 24 Warwick Lane, Paternoster Row.

Windsor Series of Poetical Anthologies.

Printed on Antique Paper. Crown 8vo. Bound in Blue Cloth,
each with suitable Emblematic Design on Cover, Price 3s. 6d.
Also in various Calf and Morocco Bindings.

Women's Voices. An Anthology of the
most Characteristic Poems by English, Scotch, and Irish Women.
Edited by Mrs. William Sharp.

Sonnets of this Century. With an
Exhaustive and Critical Essay on the Sonnet. Edited by
William Sharp.

The Children of the Poets. An Anthology
from English and American Writers of Three Centuries. Edited
by Professor Eric S. Robertson.

Sacred Song. A Volume of Religious
Verse. Selected and arranged, with Notes, by Samuel
Waddington.

A Century of Australian Song. Selected
and Edited by Douglas B. W. Sladen, B.A., Oxon.

Jacobite Songs and Ballads. Selected
and Edited, with Notes, by G. S. Macquoid.

Irish Minstrelsy. Edited, with Notes and
Introduction, by H. Halliday Sparling.

The Sonnets of Europe. A Volume of
Translations. Selected and arranged, with Notes, by Samuel
Waddington.

Early English and Scottish Poetry.
Selected and Edited, with Introduction and Notes, by H.
Macaulay Fitzgibbon.

Ballads of the North Countrie. Edited,
with Introduction, by Graham R. Tomson.

Songs and Poems of the Sea. An
Anthology of Poems Descriptive of the Sea. Edited by Mrs.
William Sharp.

Songs and Poems of Fairyland. An
Anthology of English Fairy Poetry, selected and arranged, with
an Introduction, by Arthur Edward Waite.

London: Walter Scott, 24 Warwick Lane, Paternoster Row

Recent Volumes of Verse.

ROMANTIC BALLADS AND POEMS OF PHANTASY.

By WILLIAM SHARP. SECOND EDITION. 3s.

Author of "The Human Inheritance," "Earth's Voices," "Dante Gabriel Rossetti: a Record and a Study," "Shelley: A Biographical Study," "Life of Heine," etc., etc.

"Verse of this kind is so exceptional that one can only speak of it in terms of grateful appreciation. We shall naturally look for more of the same quality from the same source; but no fountain, however affluent, yields such streams every day."—*The Academy.*

CAROLS, SONGS, AND BALLADS.

By JOSEPH SKIPSEY. (New Edition.) Crown 8vo, blue cloth, 3s. 6d.

"Mr. Skipsey can find music for every mood, whether he is dealing with the real experiences of the pitman, or with the imaginative experiences of the poet, and his verse has a rich vitality about it. In these latter days of shallow rhymes, it is pleasant to come across some one to whom poetry is a passion, not a profession."—*Pall Mall Gazette.*

DEATH'S DISGUISES AND OTHER SONNETS.

By FRANK T. MARZIALS. Parchment limp, 3/-

"Mr. Frank T. Marzials' charming and finely wrought little book of poems."
—*Scotsman.*

"IT IS THYSELF."

By MARK ANDRÉ RAFFALOVICH, Author of "In Fancy Dress," "Cyril and Lionel," etc. Crown 8vo, 3/6.

CHARACTERISTICS OF GENIUS: A POPULAR ESSAY.

By CHARLES GIBSON, M.D., Lecturer and Examiner in the Faculty of Medicine of the University of Durham. Crown 8vo, blue cloth, 3s. 6d.

London: WALTER SCOTT, 24 Warwick Lane, Paternoster Row.

THE OXFORD LIBRARY.

Strongly Bound in Elegant Cloth Binding, Price 2s. each.

This Series of Popular Books comprises many original Novels by new Authors, as well as the most choice works of Dickens, Lytton, Smollett, Scott, Ferrier, etc.

The following are now ready, and will be followed by others shortly:—

BARNABY RUDGE.

OLD CURIOSITY SHOP.

PICKWICK PAPERS.

NICHOLAS NICKLEBY.

OLIVER TWIST.

MARTIN CHUZZLEWIT.

SKETCHES BY BOZ.

RODERICK RANDOM.

PEREGRINE PICKLE.

IVANHOE.

KENILWORTH.

JACOB FAITHFUL.

PETER SIMPLE.

PAUL CLIFFORD.

EUGENE ARAM.

ERNEST MALTRAVERS.

ALICE; or, the Mysteries.

RIENZI.

PELHAM.

LAST DAYS OF POMPEII.

THE SCOTTISH CHIEFS.

WILSON'S TALES.

THE INHERITANCE.

ETHEL LINTON.

A MOUNTAIN DAISY.

HAZEL; or, Perilpoint Lighthouse.

VICAR OF WAKEFIELD.

PRINCE of the HOUSE of DAVID.

WIDE, WIDE WORLD.

VILLAGE TALES.

BEN-HUR.

UNCLE TOM'S CABIN.

ROBINSON CRUSOE.

CHARLES O'MALLEY.

MIDSHIPMAN EASY.

BRIDE OF LAMMERMOOR.

HEART OF MIDLOTHIAN.

LAST OF THE BARONS.

OLD MORTALITY.

TOM CRINGLE'S LOG.

CRUISE OF THE MIDGE.

COLLEEN BAWN.

VALENTINE VOX.

NIGHT AND MORNING.

FOXE'S BOOK OF MARTYRS.

BUNYAN'S PILGRIM'S PROGRESS

London : WALTER SCOTT, 24 Warwick Lane, Paternoster Row

THE YOUNG FOLK'S LIBRARY.

F'cap. 8vo, Cloth Elegant, Plain Edges, 1s. 6d.   Gilt Edges, 2s.

An admirable Series for the Family or for School Libraries.
Splendidly Illustrated.

Miss Matty ; or, Our Youngest Passenger.   By Mrs.
George Cupples.   And other Tales.   Illustrated.

Horace Hazelwood ; or, Little Things.   By R. Hope
Moncrieff.   And other Tales.   Illustrated.

Found Afloat.   By Mrs. George Cupples.   And other
Tales.   Illustrated.

The White Roe of Glenmere.   By Mrs. Bickerstaffe.
And other Tales.   Illustrated.

Jessie Oglethorpe : The Story of a Daughter's Devotion.   By W. H. Davenport Adams.   And other Tales.   Illustrated.

Paul and Marie, the Orphans of Auvergne.   And
other Tales.   Illustrated.

Archie Mason : An Irish Story.   By Letitia
M'Clintock.   And other Tales.   Illustrated.

The Woodfords : An Emigrant Story.   By Mrs.
Cupples.   And other Tales.   Illustrated.

Old Andy's Money : An Irish Story.   By Letitia
M'Clintock.   And other Tales.   Illustrated.

Marius Flaminius : A Story of the Days of Hadrian.
By Anna J. Buckland.   And other Tales.   Illustrated.

The Inundation of the Rhine.   From the German.
And other Tales.   Illustrated.

The Little Orphans.   From the German.   And other
Tales.   Illustrated.

Select Christian Biographies.   By Rev. Jas. Gardner,
A.M., M.D.   Illustrated.

Leoline ; or, Captured and Rescued.   By Emily
Grace Harding.

Life of David Livingstone.   By James Donald
F.R.G.S.

London : WALTER SCOTT, 24 Warwick Lane, Paternoster Row.

SCOTCH POETS IN THE
CANTERBURY SERIES.

Each in One Volume, Cloth, cut or uncut, 1s.

JACOBITE SONGS AND BALLADS.
Selected, with Notes and Introduction, by G. S. Macquoid.

"The selection is excellent, and the accompanying 'notes' exactly what is wanted in such a book."—*Arbroath Herald.*

JAMES HOGG, the Ettrick Shepherd.
Selected. Edited, with Introduction, by the Poet's Daughter, Mrs. Garden.

"The reader may be assured that he has here the finest and most characteristic work of James Hogg."—*Oxford Times.*

ALLAN RAMSAY. With Biographical
Sketch by J. Logie Robertson, M.A.

"The reading public have now what they had not before—a cheap and well-appointed edition of Ramsay, which gives all his best work and nothing but his best."—*Scotsman.*

SIR WALTER SCOTT.—MARMION, etc.
Edited, with Prefatory Notice, by William Sharp.

SIR WALTER SCOTT —LADY OF THE
LAKE, etc.

"A delightful prefatory notice."—*Derby Gazette.*

THOMAS CAMPBELL. With Introductory
Notice by John Hogben.

"The introductory essay is all that such a notice should be. The little volume is a good one, and handy for the pocket."—*The Graphic.*

ROBERT BURNS.—Poems. With Bio-
graphical Sketch by Joseph Skipsey.

ROBERT BURNS.—Songs. With Critical
Estimate by Joseph Skipsey.

"The essays are valuable additions to Burns literature, and should be read by all who are admirers of the poet, and—for that matter—by all who are not."—*Derby Gazette.*

London : WALTER SCOTT, 24 Warwick Lane, Paternoster Row.

Crown 8vo, Cloth,

PRICE ONE SHILLING.

ELOCUTION

BY

T. R. WALTON PEARSON, M.A.

Of St. Catharine's College, Cambridge,

AND

FREDERIC WILLIAM WAITHMAN,

*Lecturer on Elocution in the Leeds and
Bradford Institutes.*

London: WALTER SCOTT, 24 Warwick Lane, Paternoster Row.

Square 8vo, One Shilling.

THE NOVOCASTRIAN SERIES.

M R. WALTER SCOTT has pleasure in announcing that he has added two new exciting stories to this now very popular Series.

A WITNESS FROM THE DEAD.
By FLORENCE LAYARD.

The scene of this story is laid in Brussels, and is told by an English Special Reporter of foreign *causes célèbres*. The dead body of a young and beautiful woman, curiously contorted, in evening dress, is found one night lying on the *Champ de Mars*. A murder of peculiar atrocity of conception, as is subsequently discovered, has been committed. Those engaged in tracking the unknown murderer are constantly conscious of being subject to peculiar mesmeric influences, and through some occult agency of psychical reproduction, the horrible details of the murder seem to be actually re-enacted before the eyes of the French Detective and the Reporter, in the very room in which the crime was perpetrated. The tale is told with verisimilitude and power, and the multitudinous readers of shilling fiction will find in " A WITNESS FROM THE DEAD " a climax of dramatic sensation.

THE UGLY STORY OF MISS WETHERBY.
By RICHARD PRYCE, Author of " An Evil Spirit," etc.

The author has hit upon a perfectly novel plot, dealing with the adventures of one Mr. Sloane Wetherby, a Bohemian young gentleman about town, and the very peculiar methods he adopts with a view to obtain fraudulent possession of the immense fortune of an invalid widow. The story is elaborated with admirable literary skill, and the interest, excited from the beginning, is sustained without a break to the end.

London : WALTER SCOTT, 24 Warwick Lane, Paternoster Row.

www.ingramcontent.com/pod-product-compliance
Lightning Source LLC
Chambersburg PA
CBHW030558040726

47497CB00008B/2778